MORE PRAISE FOR BABYMOUSE!

"Sassy, smart . . . Babymouse is here to stay."
—The Horn Book Magazine

"Young readers will happily fall in line."
—Kirkus Reviews

"The brother-sister creative team hits the mark with humor, sweetness, and characters so genuine they can pass for real kids." —Booklist

"Babymouse is spunky, ambitious, and, at times, a total dweeb."
—School Library Journal

Treat yourself to all the **BABYMOUSE** books:

#1 BABYMOUSE: Queen of the World!
#2 BABYMOUSE: Our Hero
#3 BABYMOUSE: Beach Babe
#4 BABYMOUSE: Rock Star
#5 BABYMOUSE: Heartbreaker
#6 CAMP BABYMOUSE
#7 BABYMOUSE: Skater Girl
#8 BABYMOUSE: Puppy Love
#9 BABYMOUSE: Monster Mash
#10 BABYMOUSE: The Musical
#11 BABYMOUSE: Dragonslayer

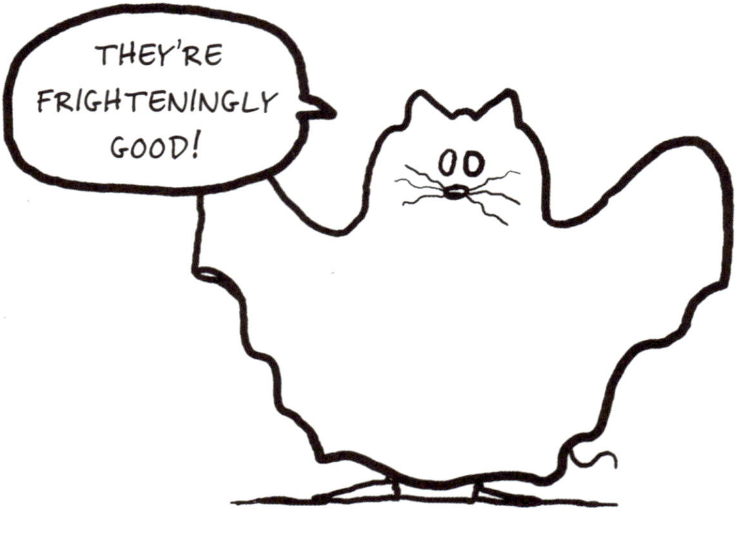
THEY'RE FRIGHTENINGLY GOOD!

BABYMOUSE
MONSTER MASH

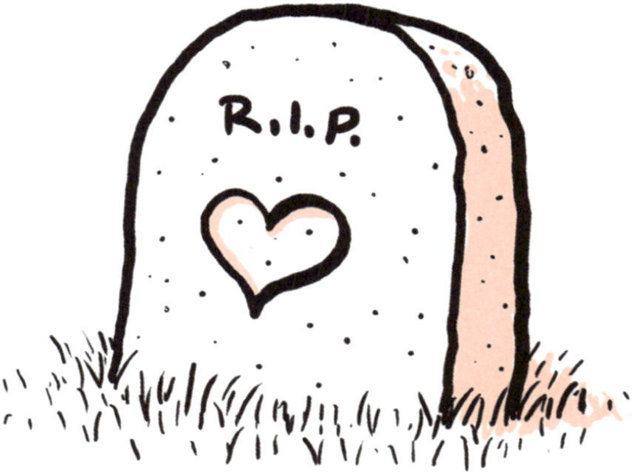
R.I.P.

BY JENNIFER L. HOLM & MATTHEW HOLM

RANDOM HOUSE NEW YORK

Copyright © 2008 by Jennifer Holm and Matthew Holm.

All rights reserved.
Published in the United States by Random House Children's Books,
a division of Random House, Inc., New York.

RANDOM HOUSE and colophon are registered trademarks of Random House, Inc.

Visit us on the Web! www.randomhouse.com/kids
www.babymouse.com

Educators and librarians, for a variety of teaching tools, visit us at
www.randomhouse.com/teachers

Library of Congress Cataloging-in-Publication Data
Holm, Jennifer L.
Babymouse : monster mash / by Jennifer L. Holm & Matthew Holm. — 1st ed.
   p. cm.
Summary: A graphic novel following the Halloween adventures of Babymouse, an
imaginative young mouse.
ISBN 978-0-375-84387-7 (trade) — ISBN 978-0-375-93789-7 (lib. bdg.)
1. Graphic novels. [1. Graphic novels. 2. Halloween—Fiction. 3. Mice—Fiction.]
I. Holm, Matthew. II. Title.
PZ7.7.H65Bam   2008   [Fic]   2008008433

PRINTED IN MALAYSIA   14 13 12 11 10 9 8 7 6 5

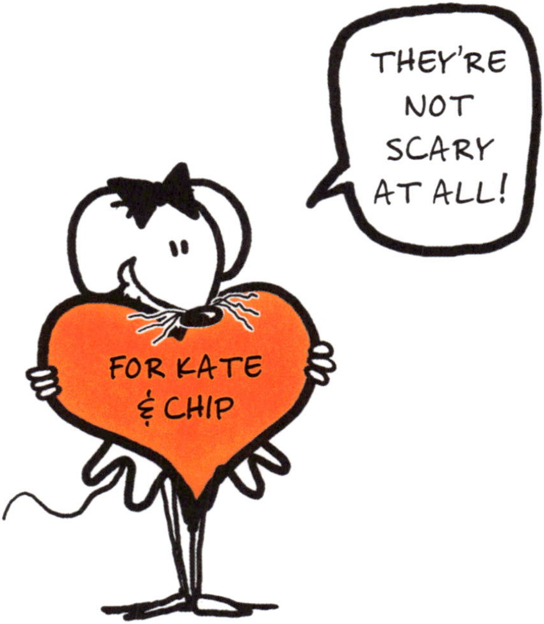
THEY'RE NOT SCARY AT ALL!
FOR KATE & CHIP

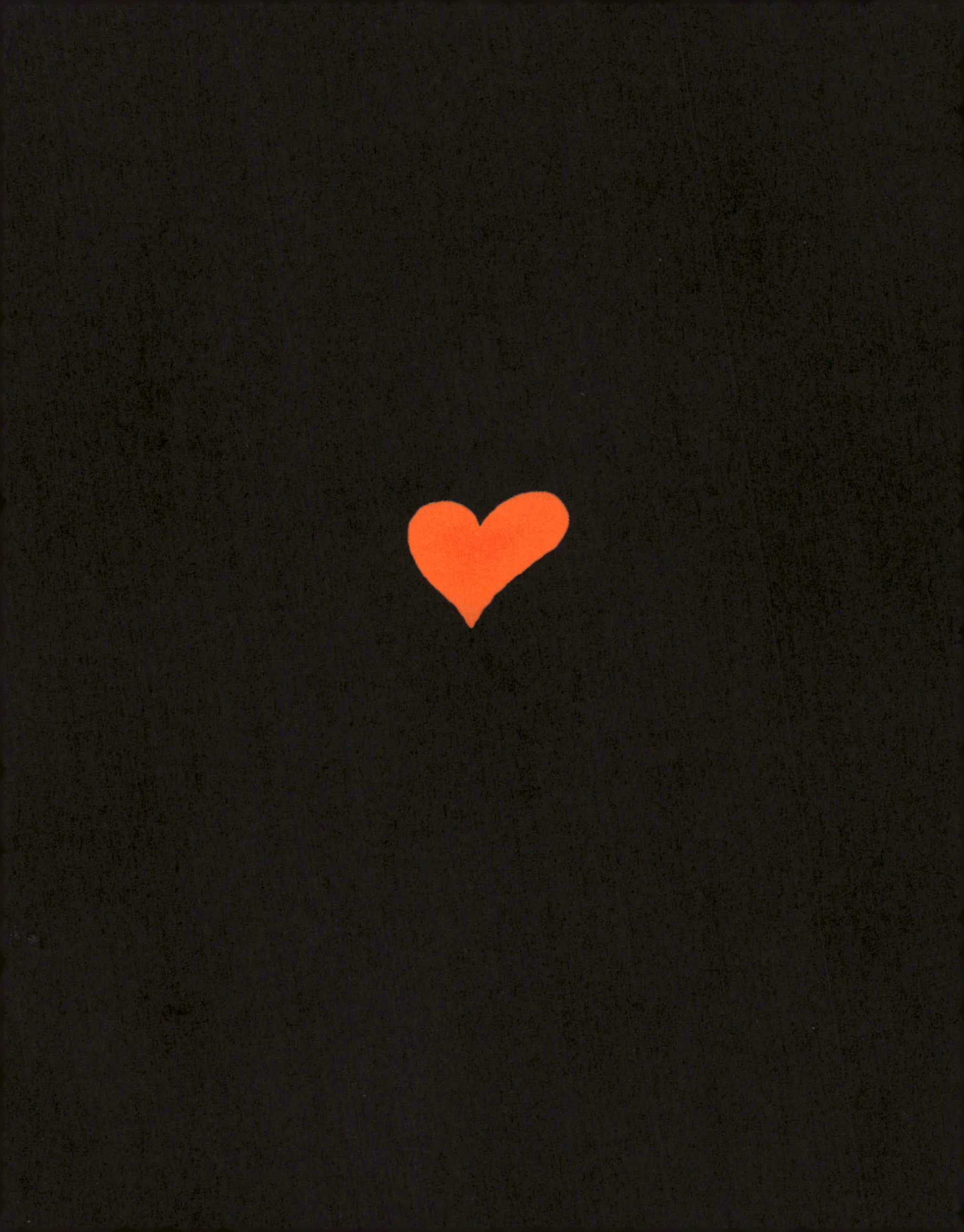

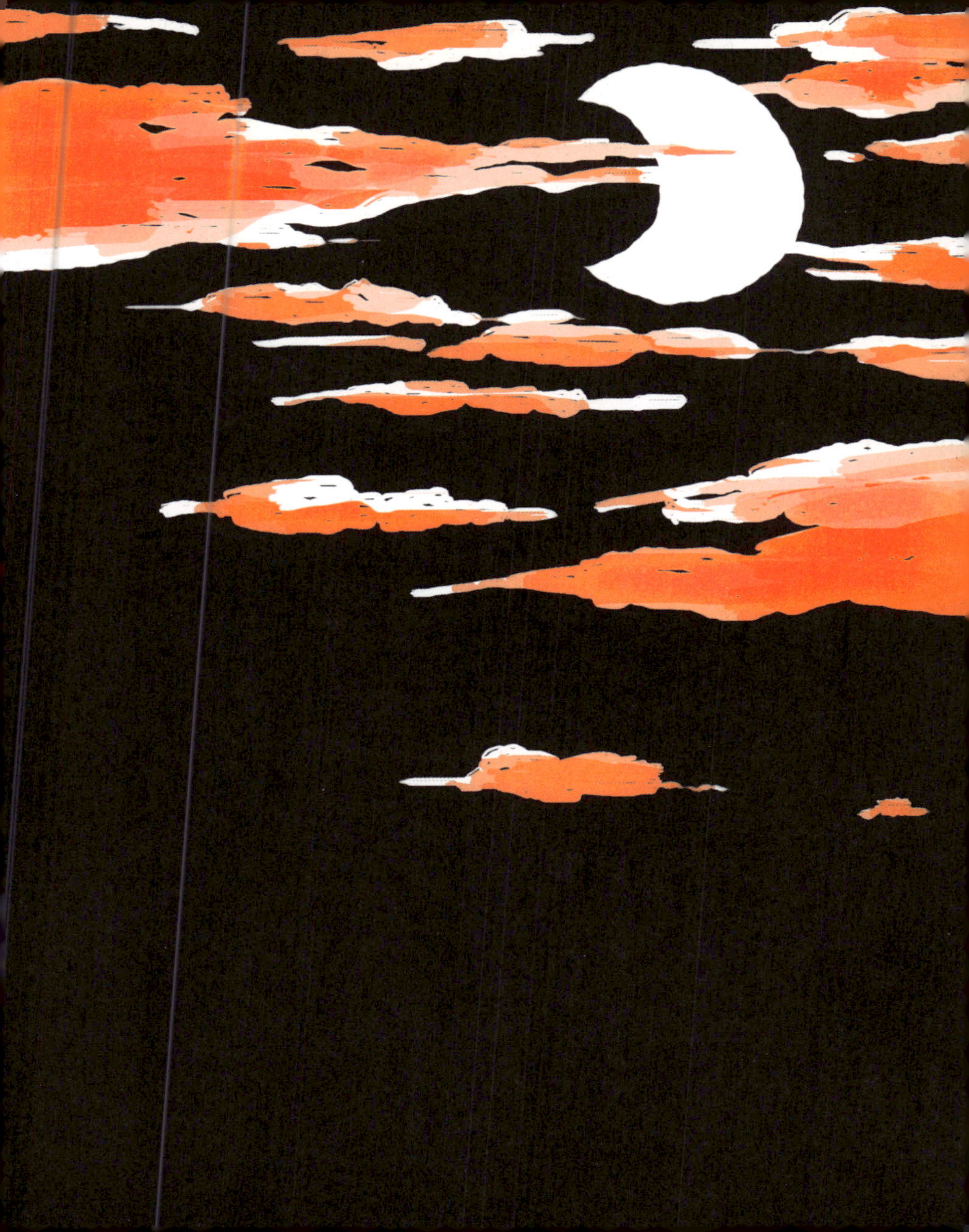

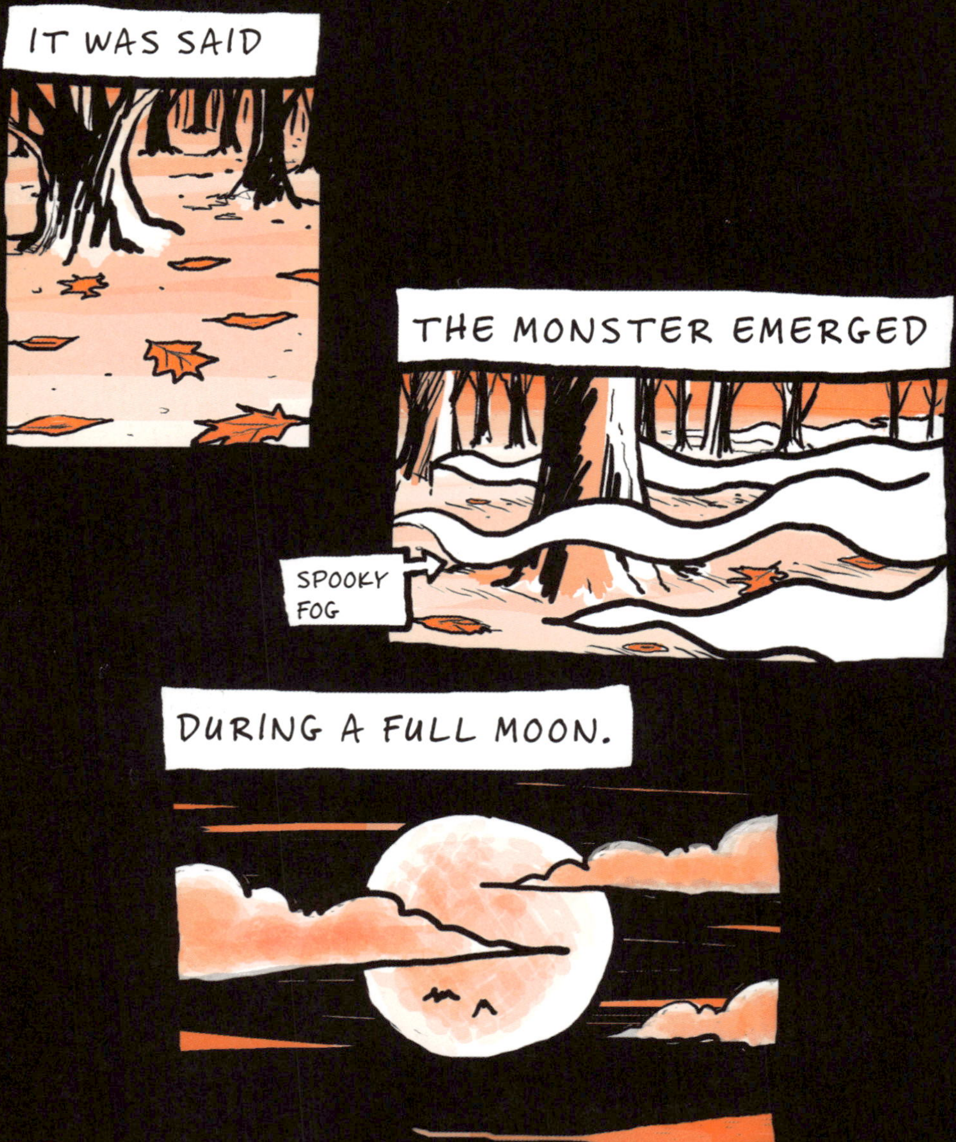
IT WAS SAID
THE MONSTER EMERGED
SPOOKY FOG
DURING A FULL MOON.

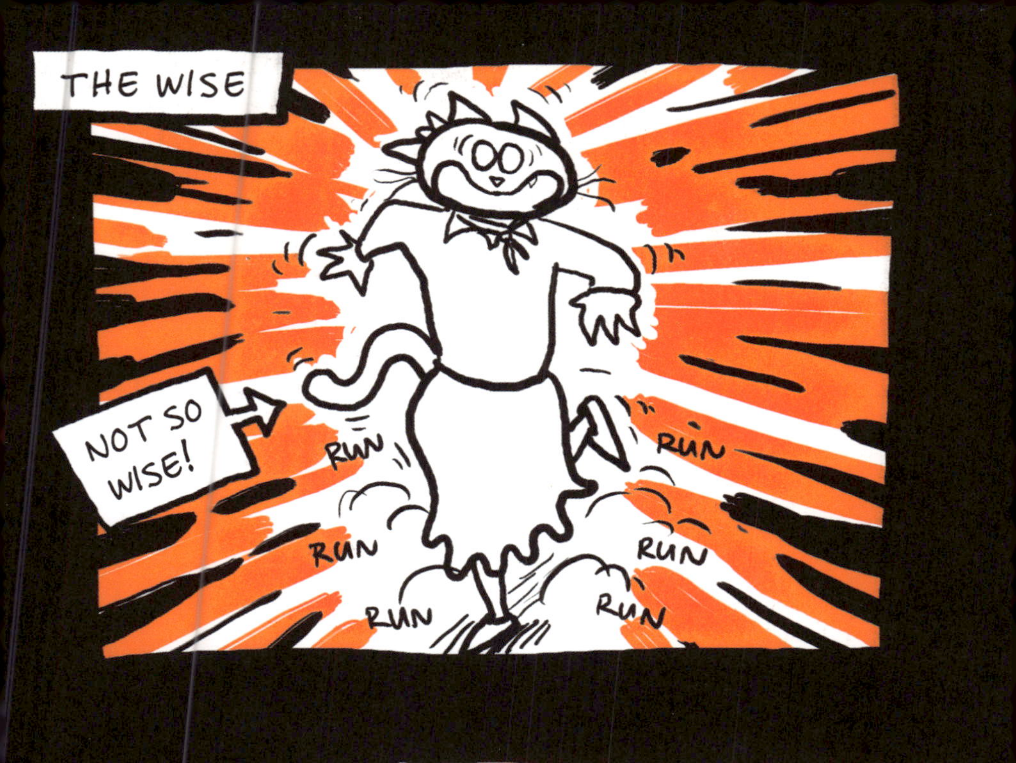
THE WISE
NOT SO WISE!
RUN
RUN
RUN
RUN
RUN
RUN

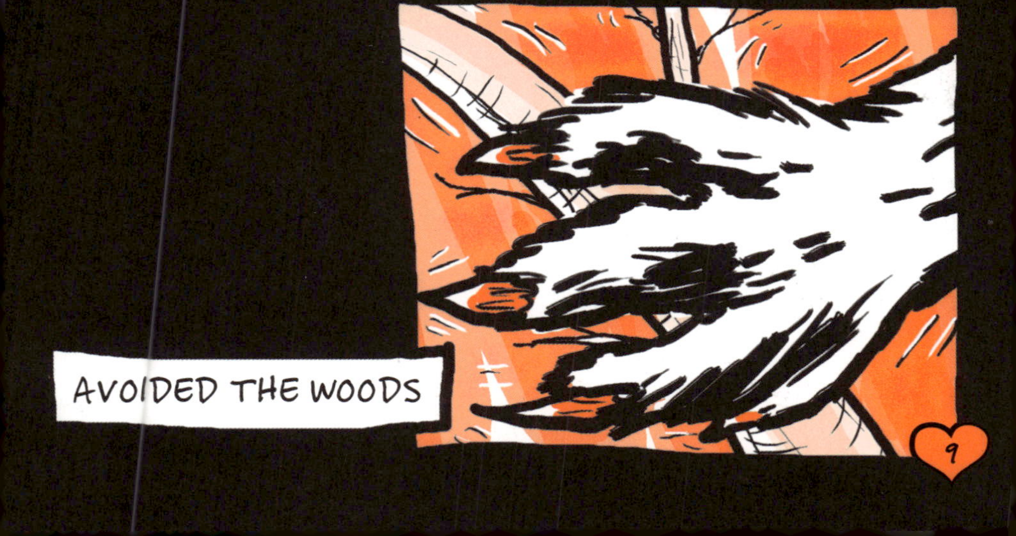
AVOIDED THE WOODS

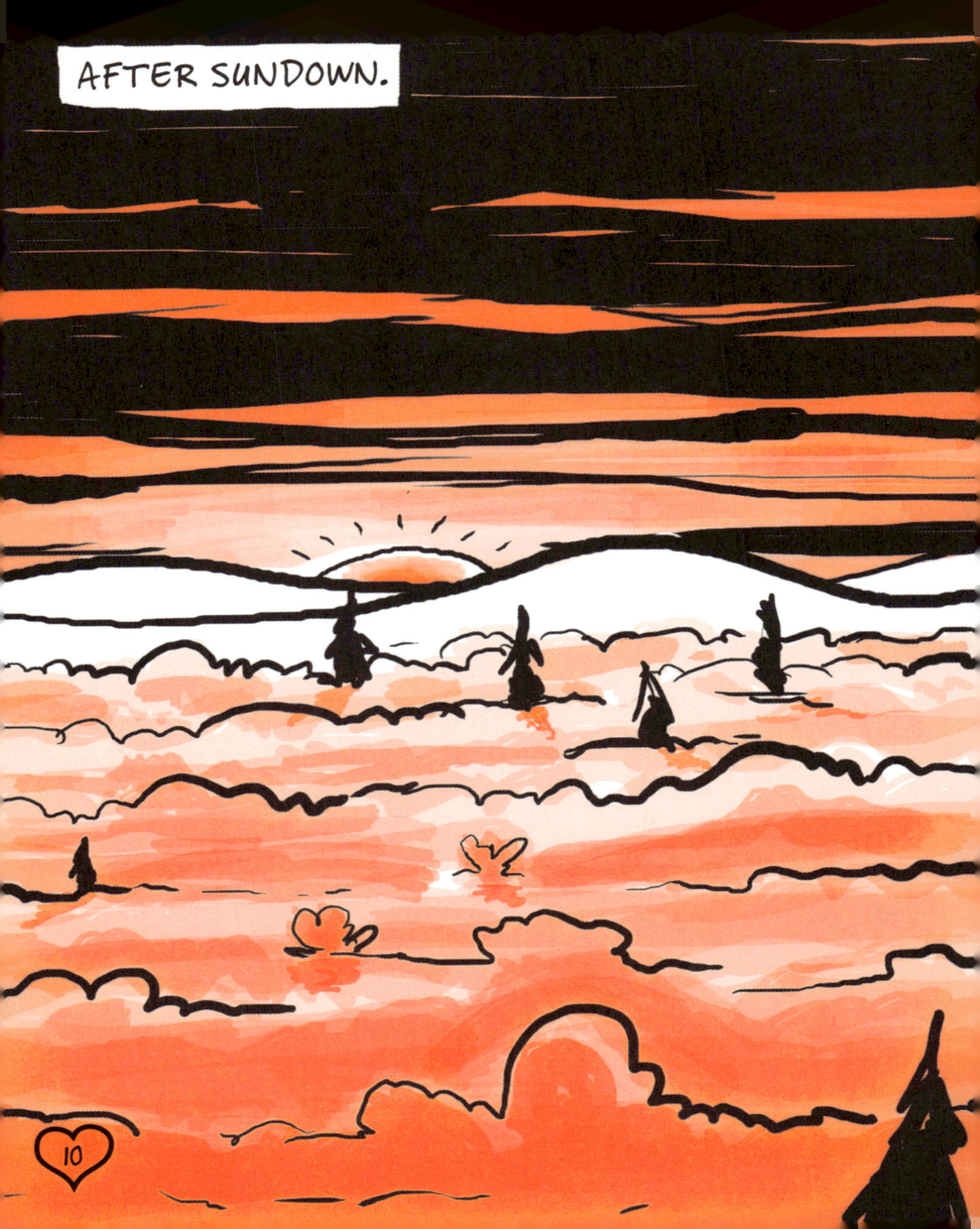
AFTER SUNDOWN.

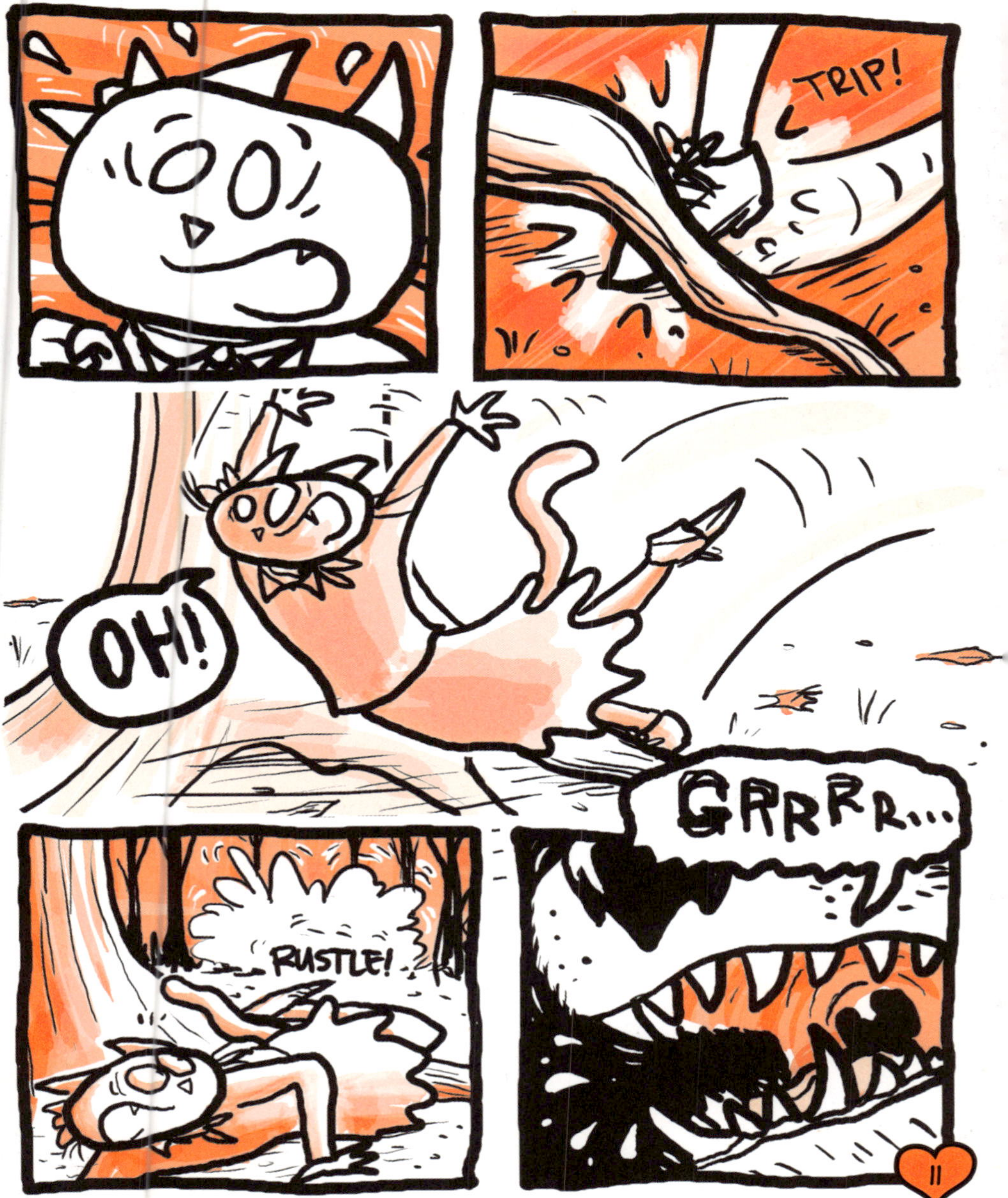
TRIP!
OH!
RUSTLE!
GRRRR...

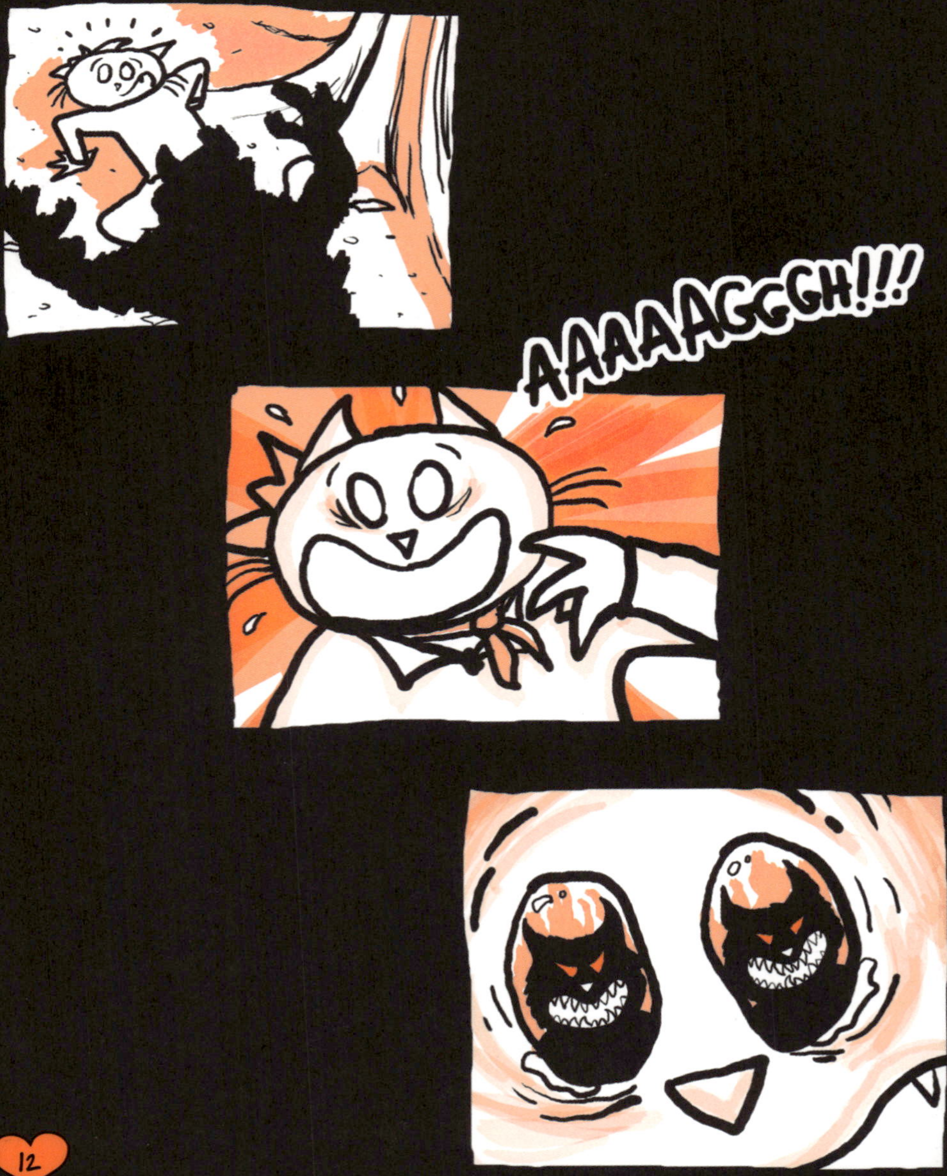
AAAAAAGGGH!!!

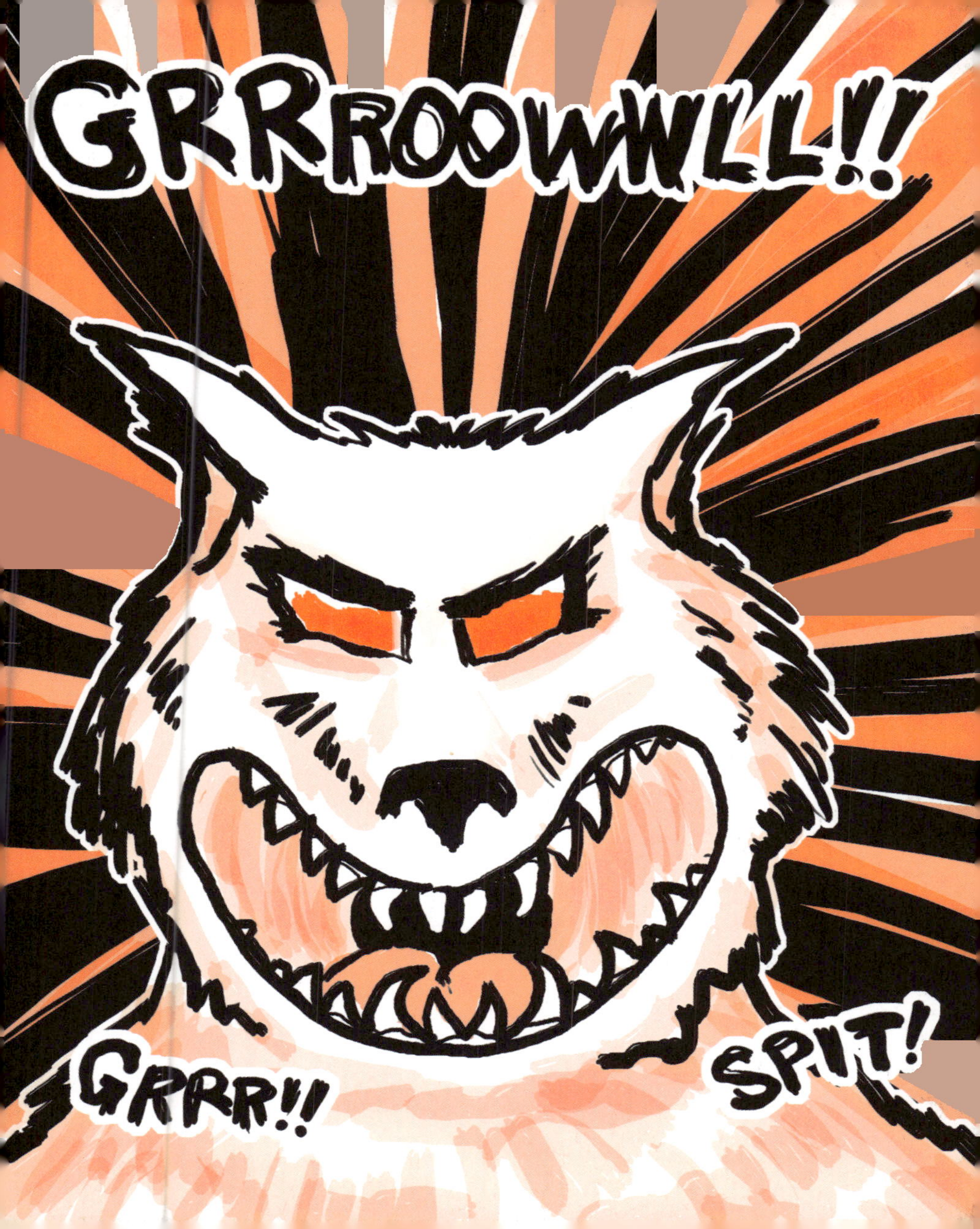
GRRROOWWLL!!
GRRR!!
SPIT!

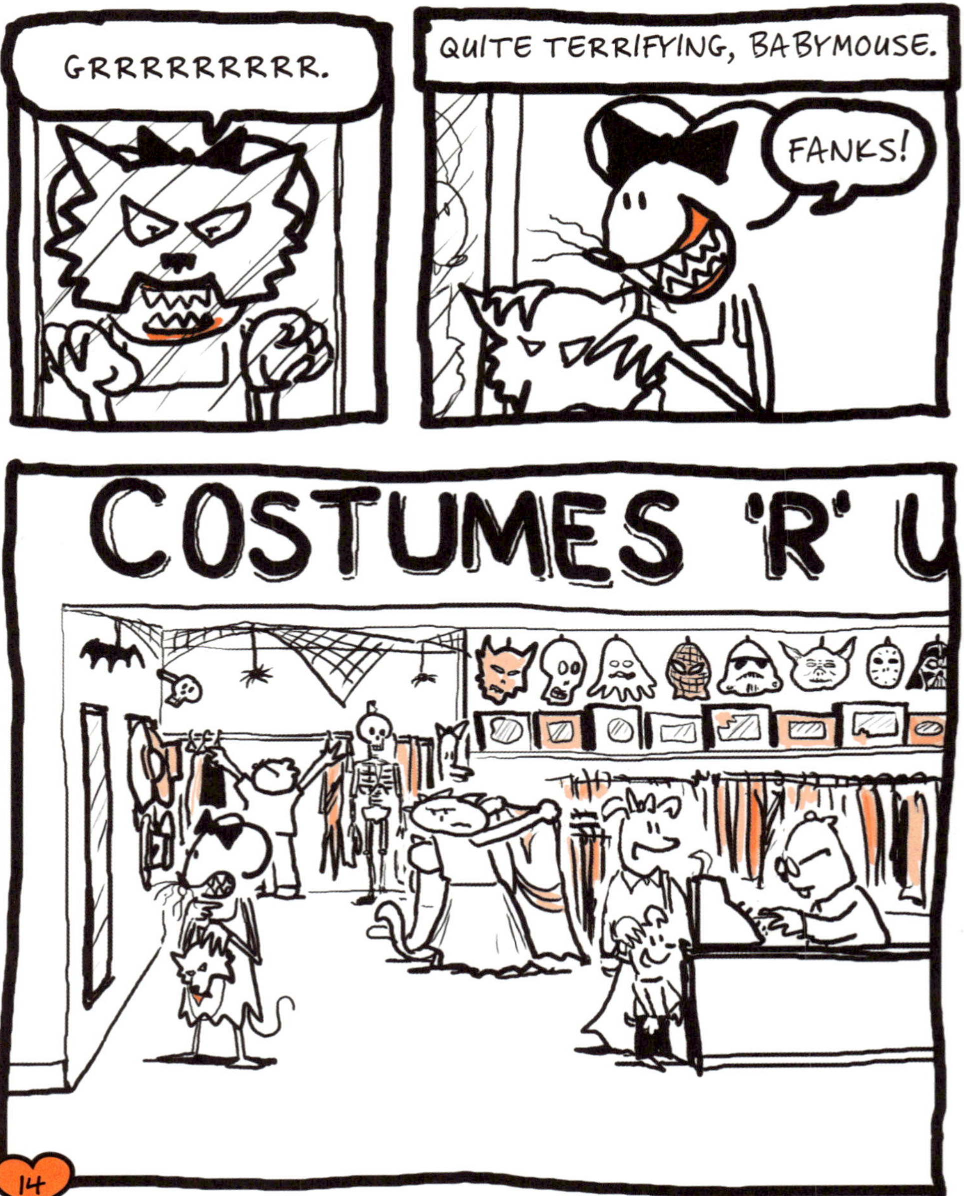
GRRRRRRRRR.
QUITE TERRIFYING, BABYMOUSE.
FANKS!
COSTUMES 'R' U

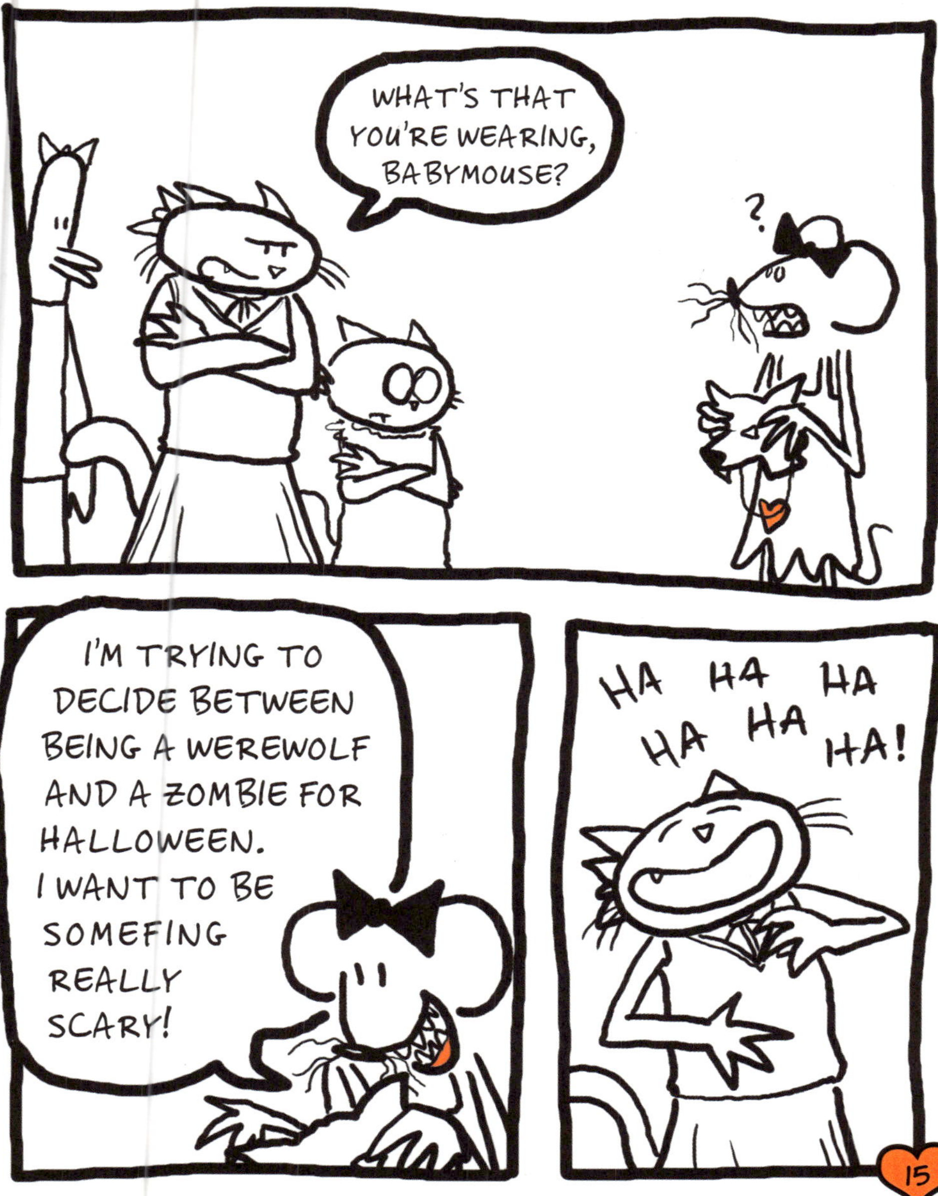
WHAT'S THAT YOU'RE WEARING, BABYMOUSE?
?
I'M TRYING TO DECIDE BETWEEN BEING A WEREWOLF AND A ZOMBIE FOR HALLOWEEN. I WANT TO BE SOMEFING REALLY SCARY!
HA HA HA HA HA HA!

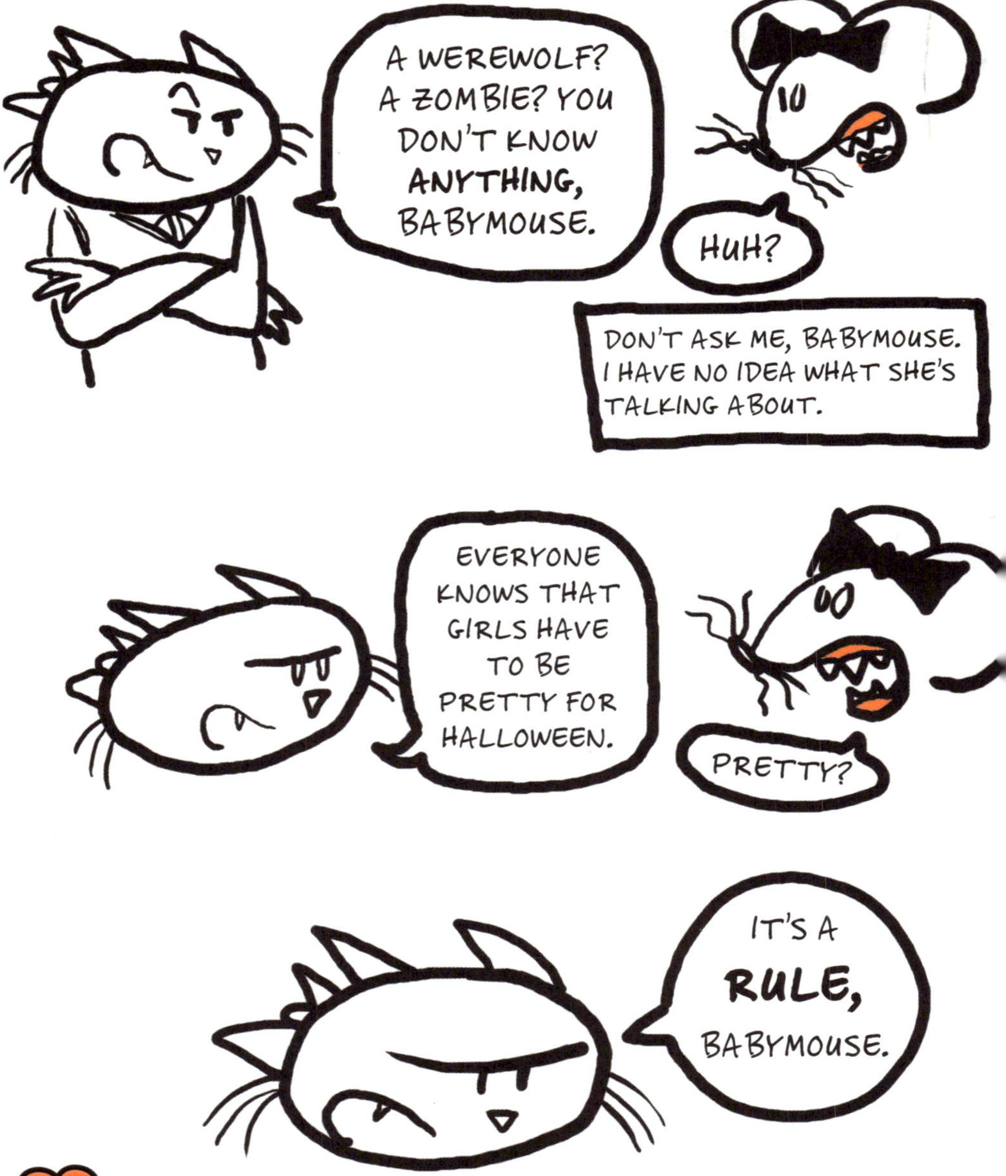
A WEREWOLF? A ZOMBIE? YOU DON'T KNOW **ANYTHING**, BABYMOUSE.
HUH?
DON'T ASK ME, BABYMOUSE. I HAVE NO IDEA WHAT SHE'S TALKING ABOUT.
EVERYONE KNOWS THAT GIRLS HAVE TO BE PRETTY FOR HALLOWEEN.
PRETTY?
IT'S A **RULE**, BABYMOUSE.

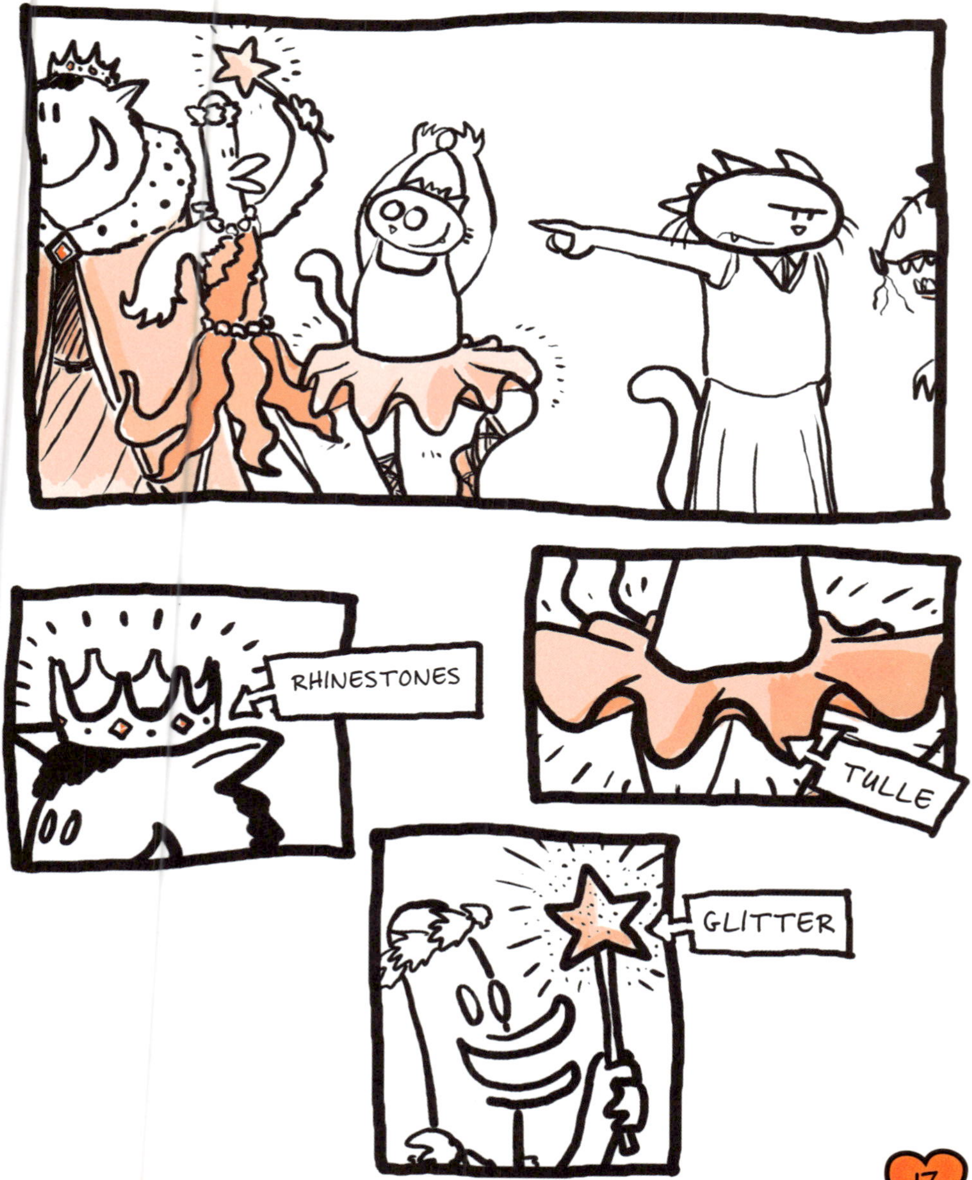
RHINESTONES
TULLE
GLITTER

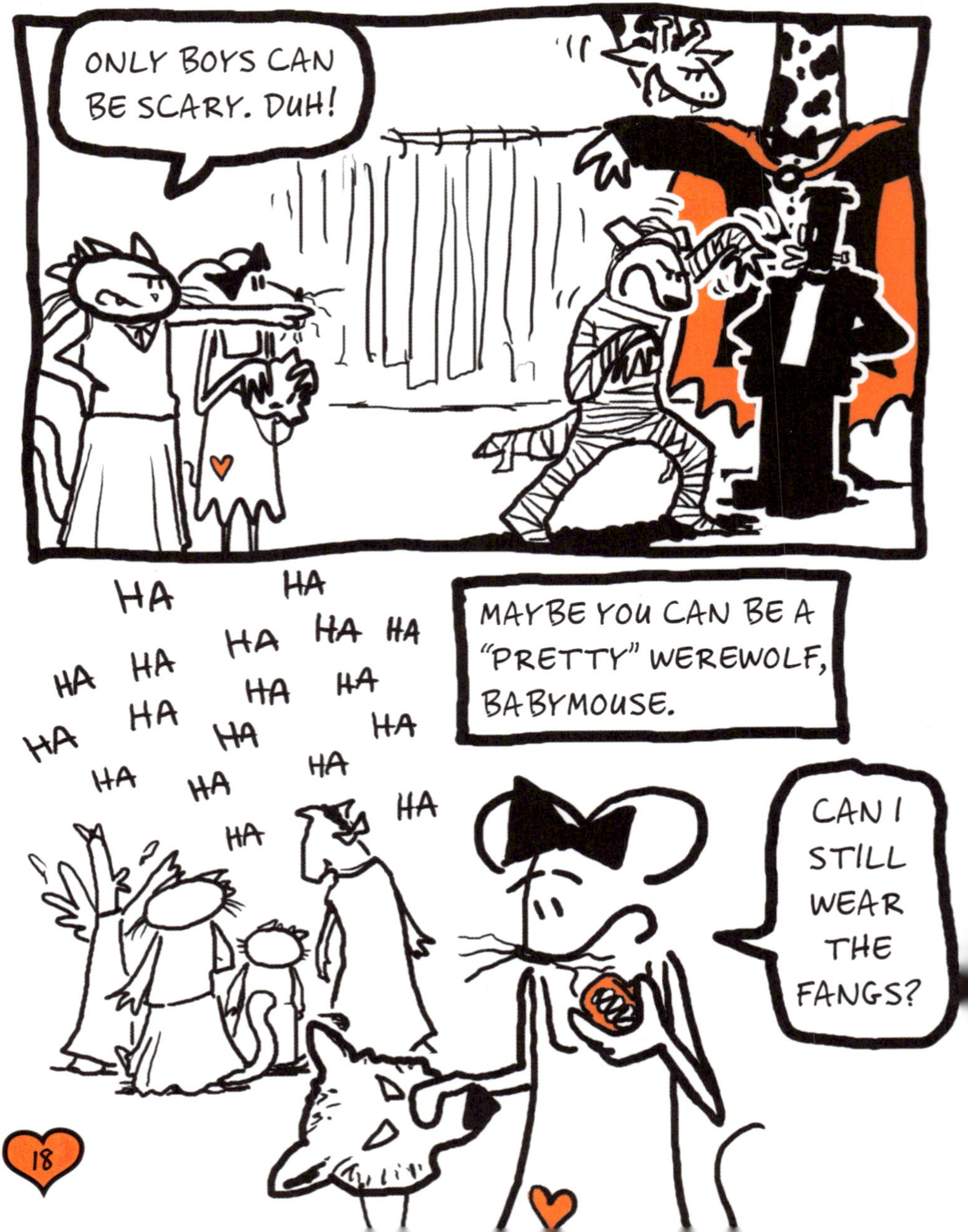
ONLY BOYS CAN BE SCARY. DUH!
HA HA HA HA HA HA HA HA HA HA HA HA HA HA HA HA HA HA
MAYBE YOU CAN BE A "PRETTY" WEREWOLF, BABYMOUSE.
CAN I STILL WEAR THE FANGS?

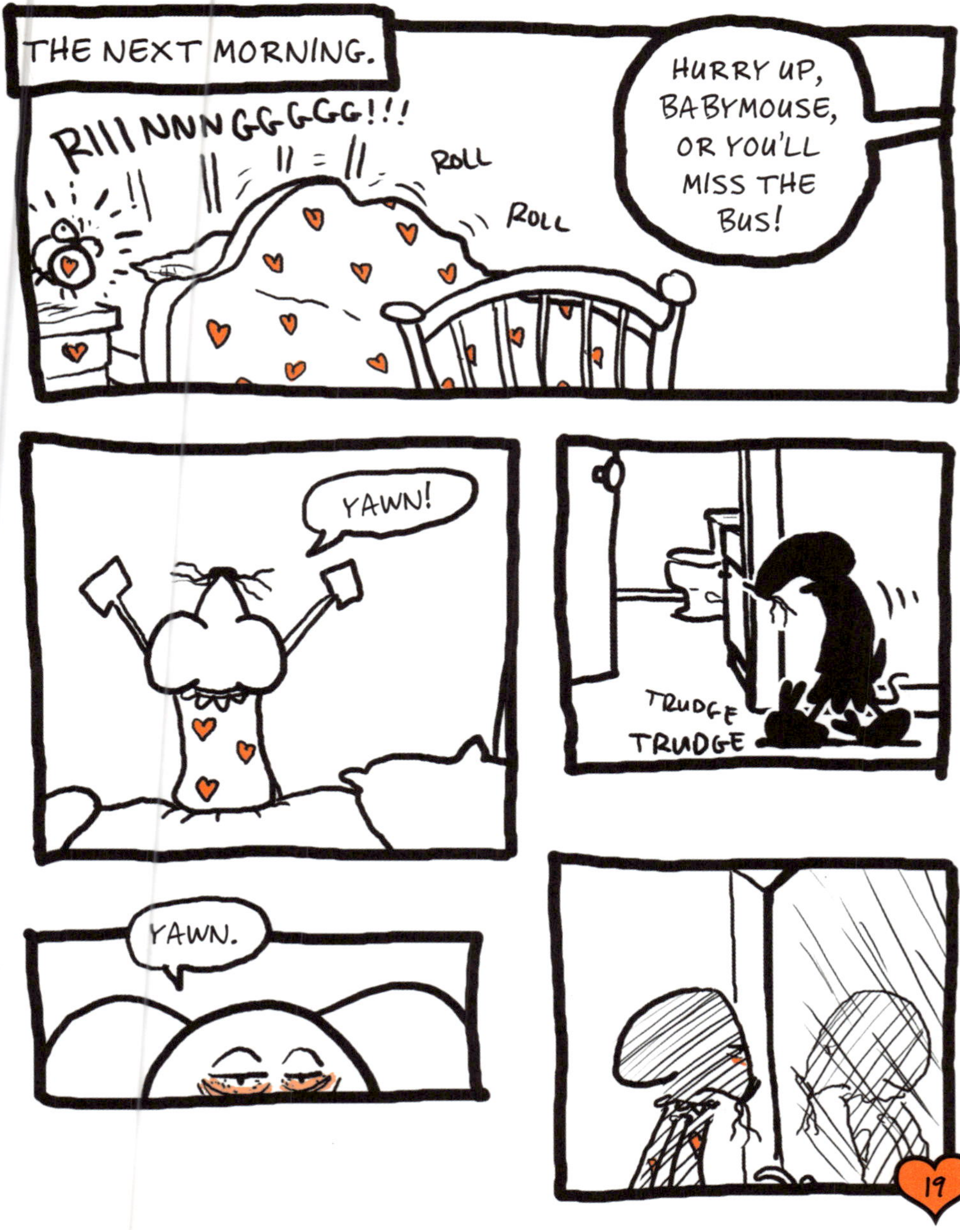
THE NEXT MORNING.
RIIINNNGGGGG!!!
ROLL
ROLL
HURRY UP, BABYMOUSE, OR YOU'LL MISS THE BUS!
YAWN!
TRUDGE
TRUDGE
YAWN.

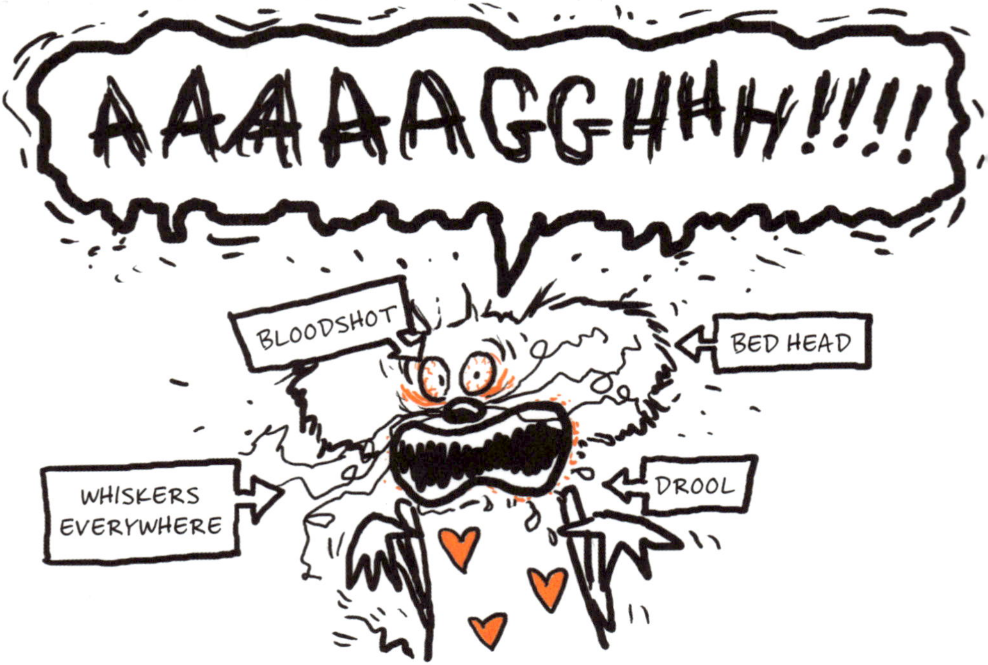
AAAAAGGHHH!!!!
BLOODSHOT
BED HEAD
WHISKERS EVERYWHERE
DROOL

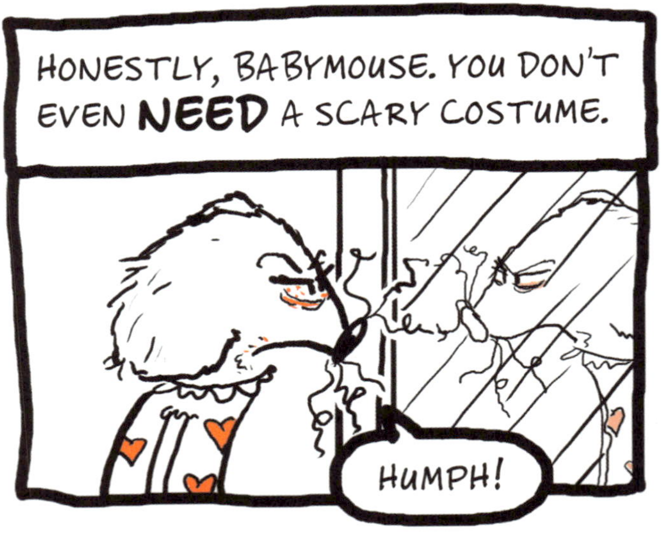
HONESTLY, BABYMOUSE. YOU DON'T EVEN **NEED** A SCARY COSTUME.
HUMPH!

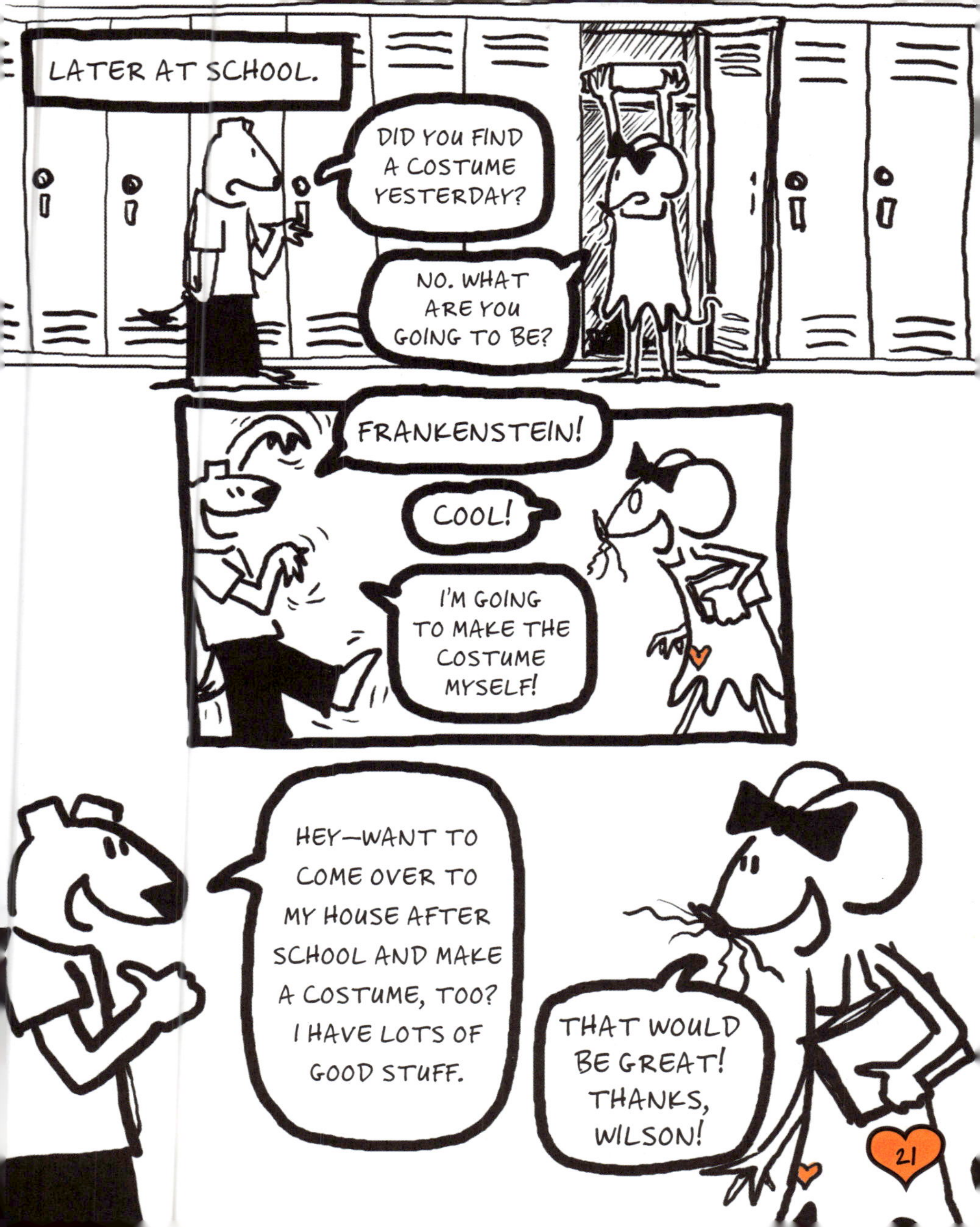

LATER AT SCHOOL.
DID YOU FIND A COSTUME YESTERDAY?
NO. WHAT ARE YOU GOING TO BE?
FRANKENSTEIN!
COOL!
I'M GOING TO MAKE THE COSTUME MYSELF!
HEY—WANT TO COME OVER TO MY HOUSE AFTER SCHOOL AND MAKE A COSTUME, TOO? I HAVE LOTS OF GOOD STUFF.
THAT WOULD BE GREAT! THANKS, WILSON!

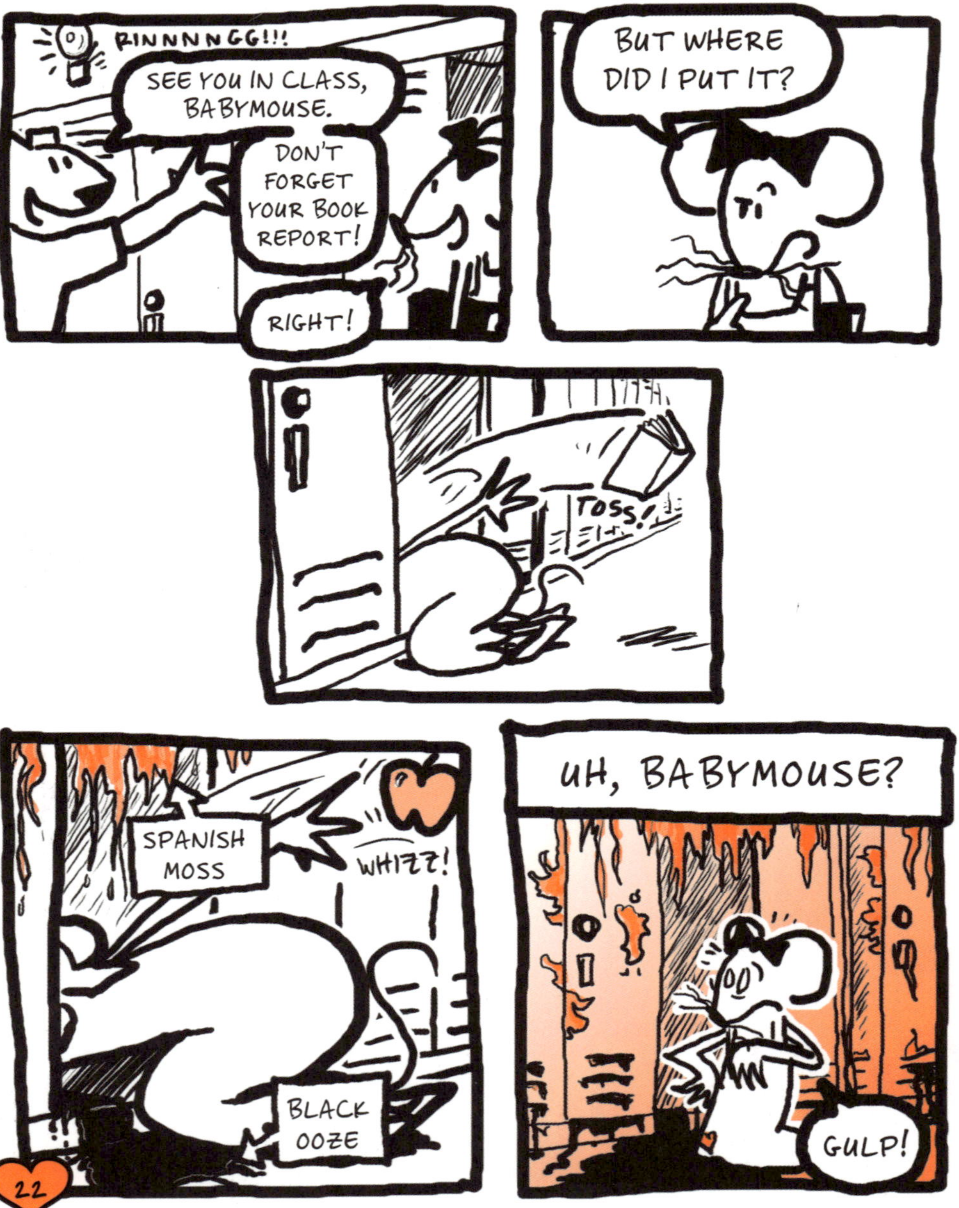
RINNNNGG!!!
SEE YOU IN CLASS, BABYMOUSE.
DON'T FORGET YOUR BOOK REPORT!
RIGHT!
BUT WHERE DID I PUT IT?
TOSS!
SPANISH MOSS
WHIZZ!
BLACK OOZE
UH, BABYMOUSE?
GULP!

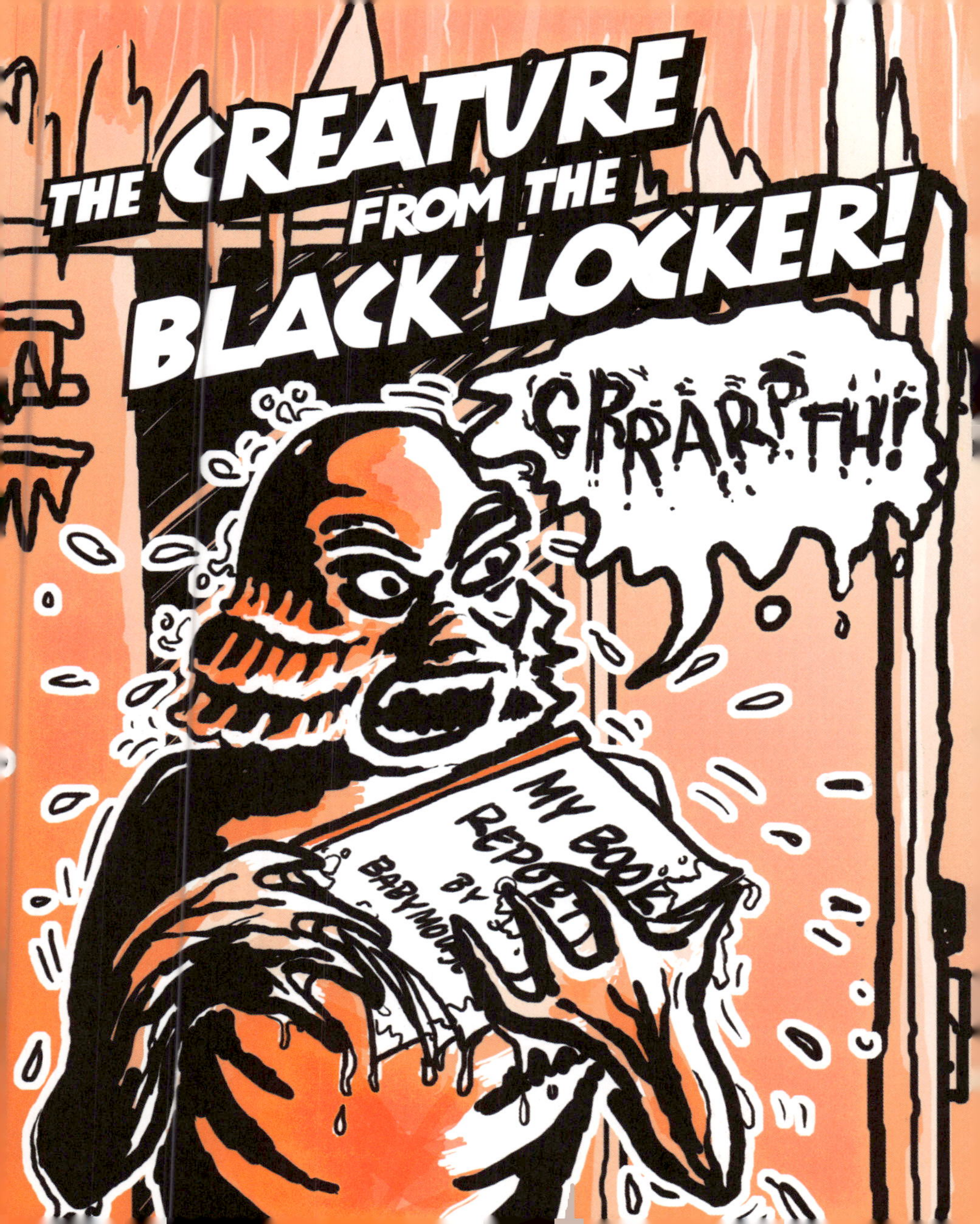
THE CREATURE FROM THE BLACK LOCKER!
GRRARPTH!
MY BOOK REPORT BY BABYMOUSE

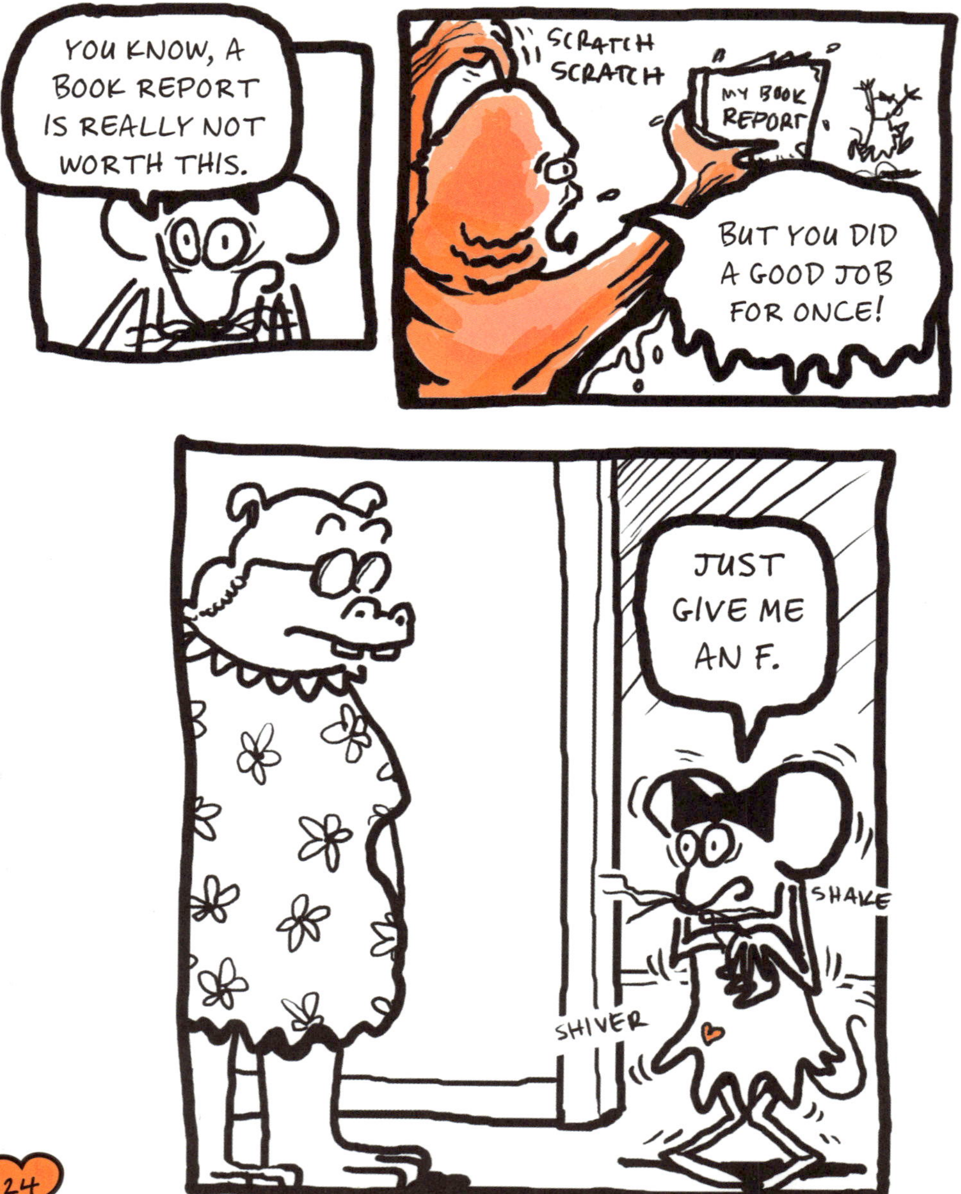
YOU KNOW, A BOOK REPORT IS REALLY NOT WORTH THIS.
SCRATCH SCRATCH
MY BOOK REPORT
BUT YOU DID A GOOD JOB FOR ONCE!
JUST GIVE ME AN F.
SHAKE
SHIVER

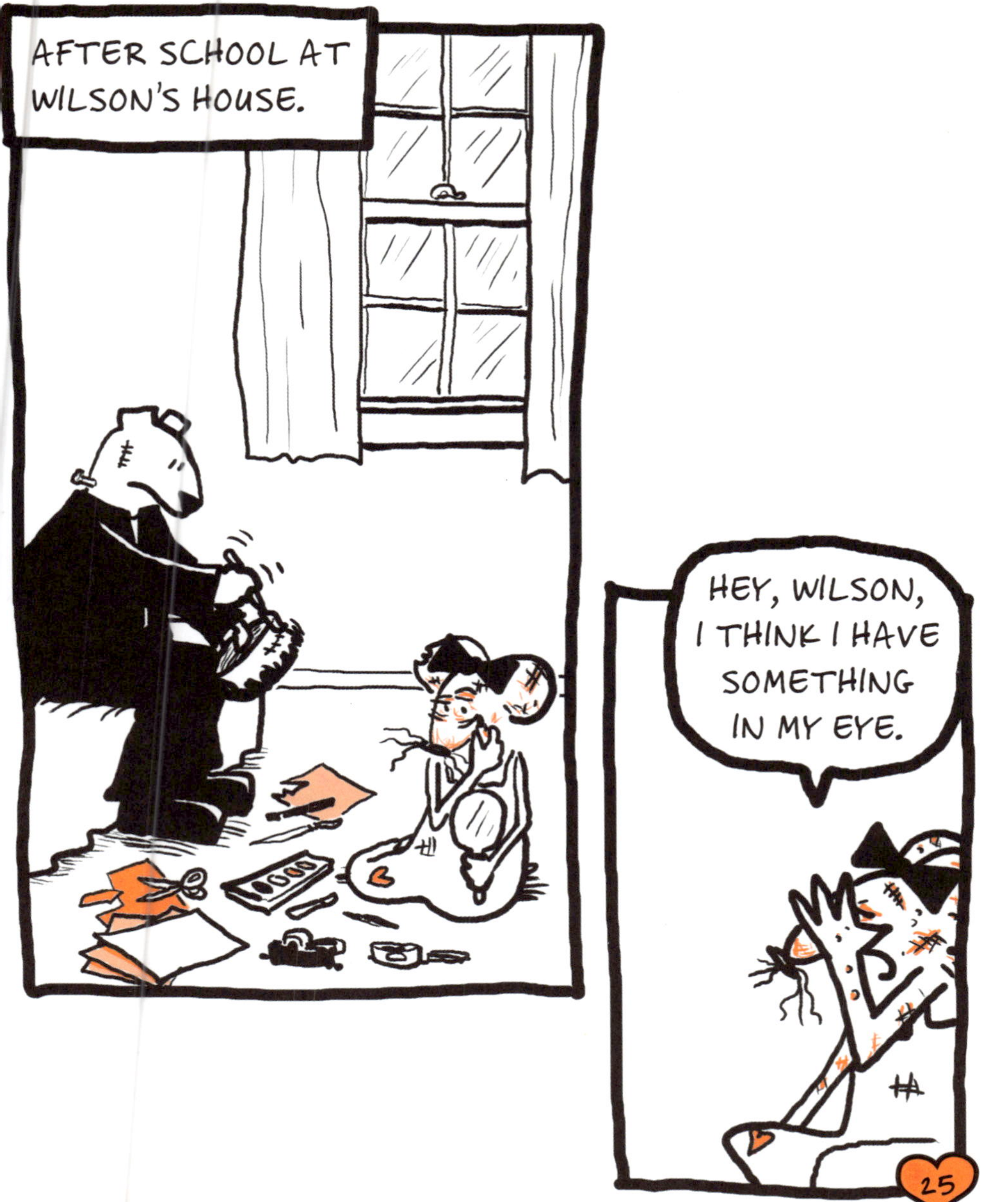
AFTER SCHOOL AT WILSON'S HOUSE.
HEY, WILSON, I THINK I HAVE SOMETHING IN MY EYE.

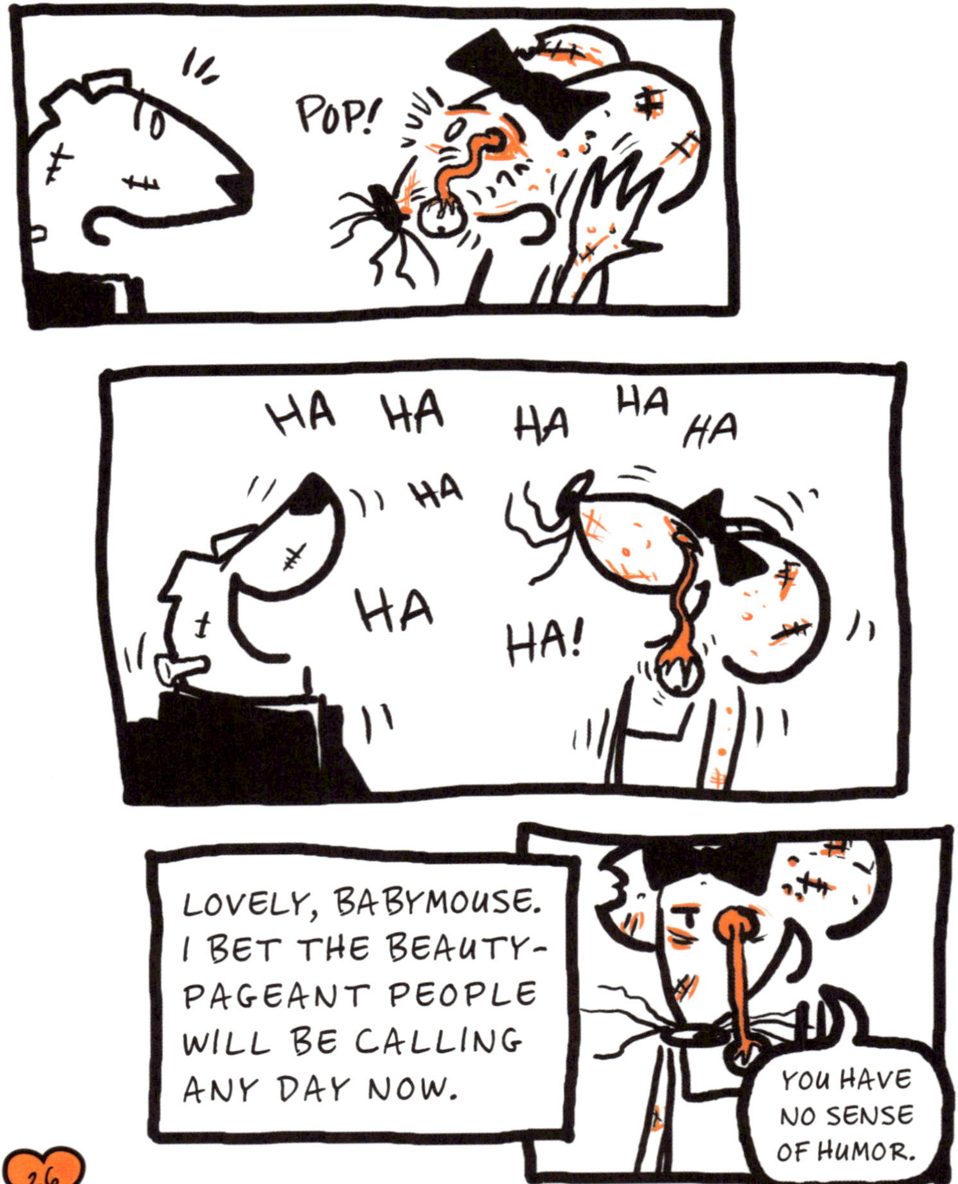
POP!
HA HA HA HA HA
HA
HA
HA!
LOVELY, BABYMOUSE. I BET THE BEAUTY-PAGEANT PEOPLE WILL BE CALLING ANY DAY NOW.
YOU HAVE NO SENSE OF HUMOR.

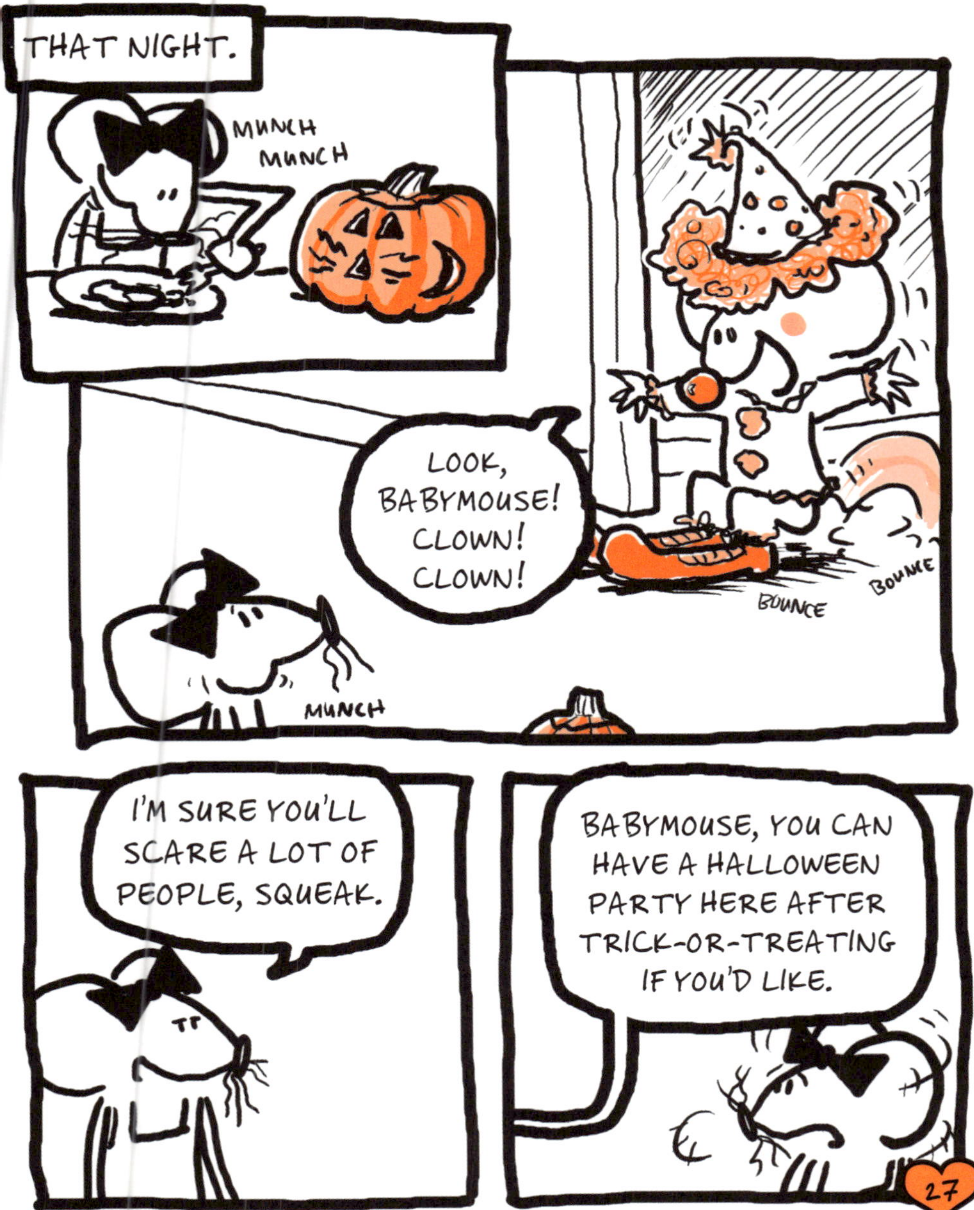
THAT NIGHT.
MUNCH MUNCH
LOOK, BABYMOUSE! CLOWN! CLOWN!
BOUNCE
BOUNCE
MUNCH
I'M SURE YOU'LL SCARE A LOT OF PEOPLE, SQUEAK.
BABYMOUSE, YOU CAN HAVE A HALLOWEEN PARTY HERE AFTER TRICK-OR-TREATING IF YOU'D LIKE.

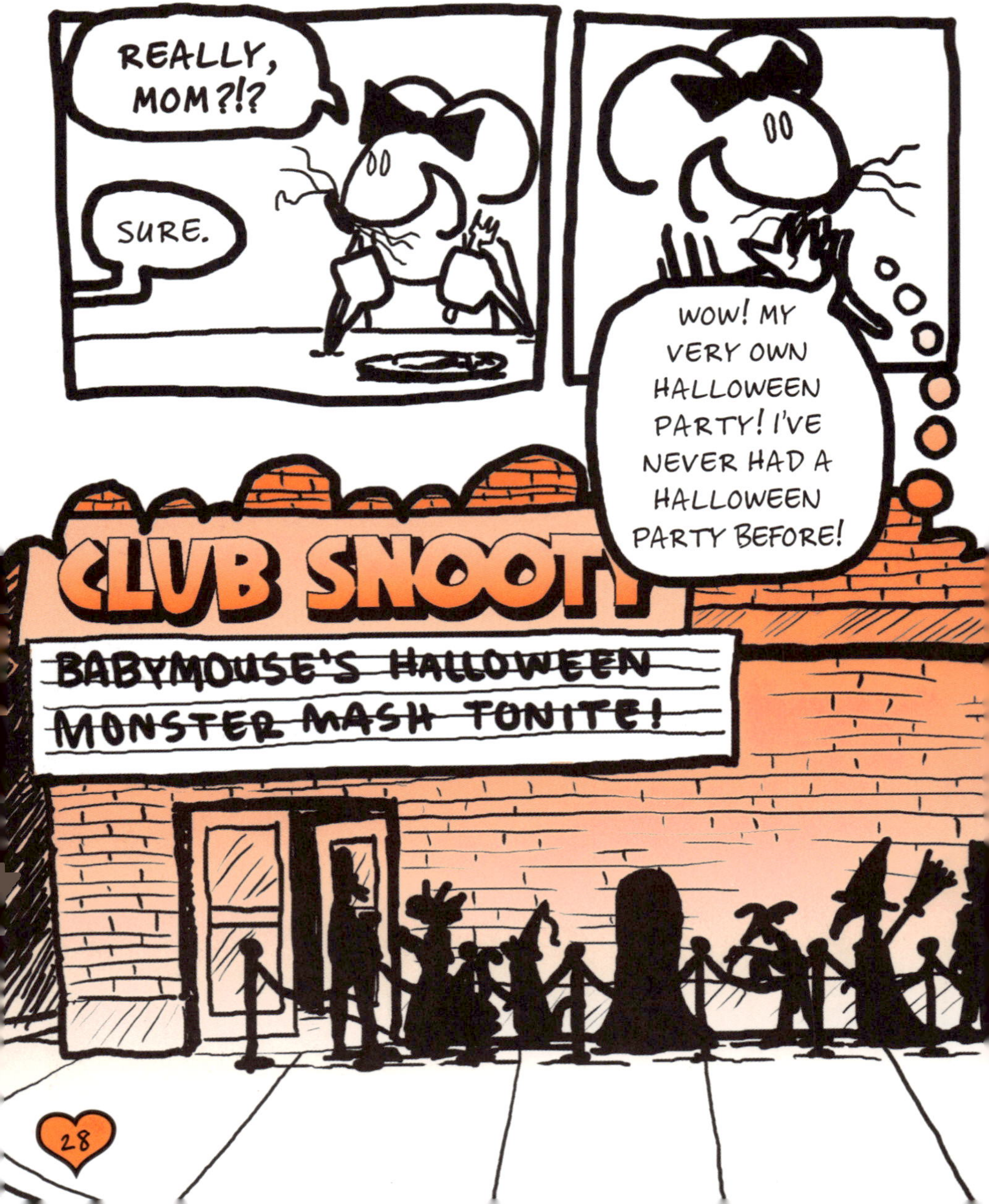
REALLY, MOM?!?
SURE.
WOW! MY VERY OWN HALLOWEEN PARTY! I'VE NEVER HAD A HALLOWEEN PARTY BEFORE!
CLUB SNOOTY
BABYMOUSE'S HALLOWEEN MONSTER MASH TONITE!

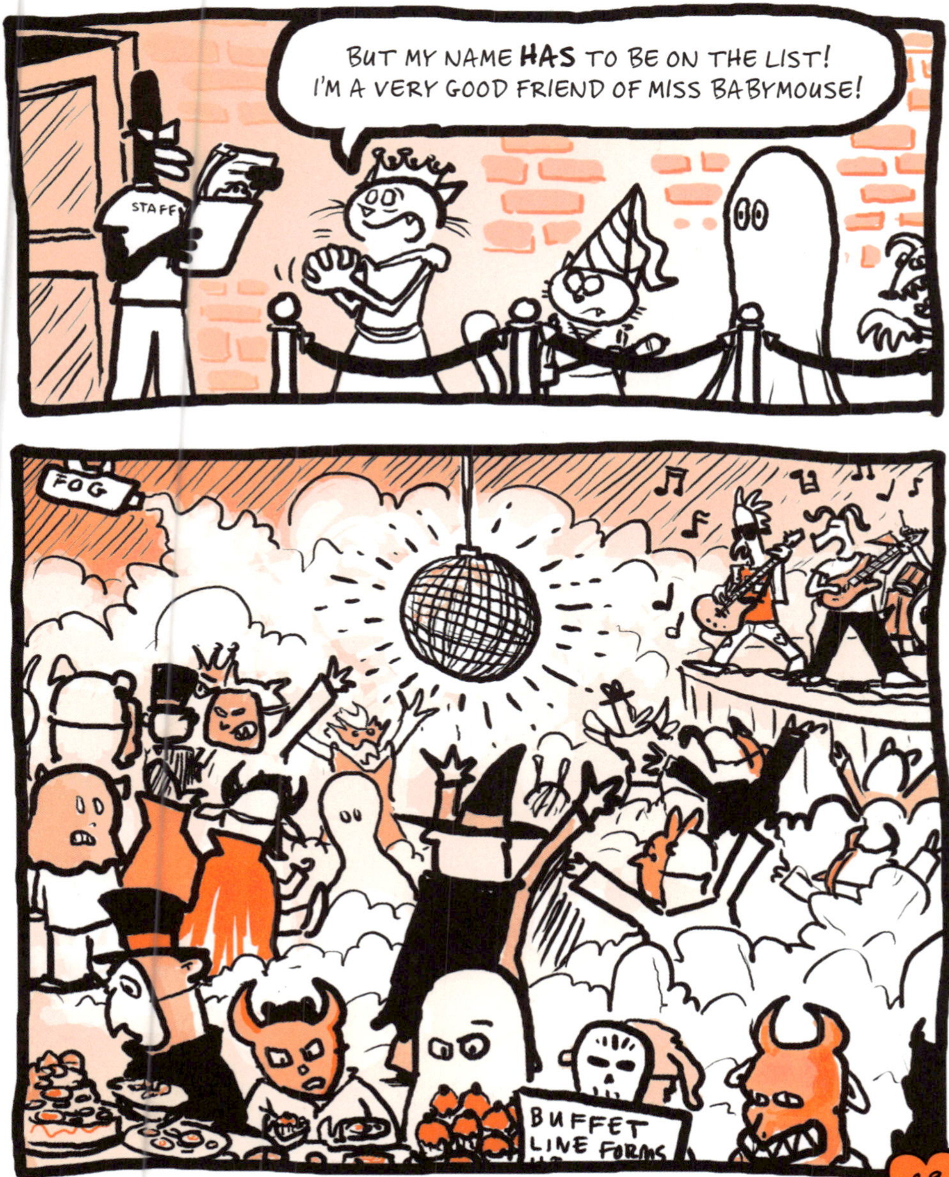
STAFF
BUT MY NAME **HAS** TO BE ON THE LIST! I'M A VERY GOOD FRIEND OF MISS BABYMOUSE!
FOG
BUFFET LINE FORMS

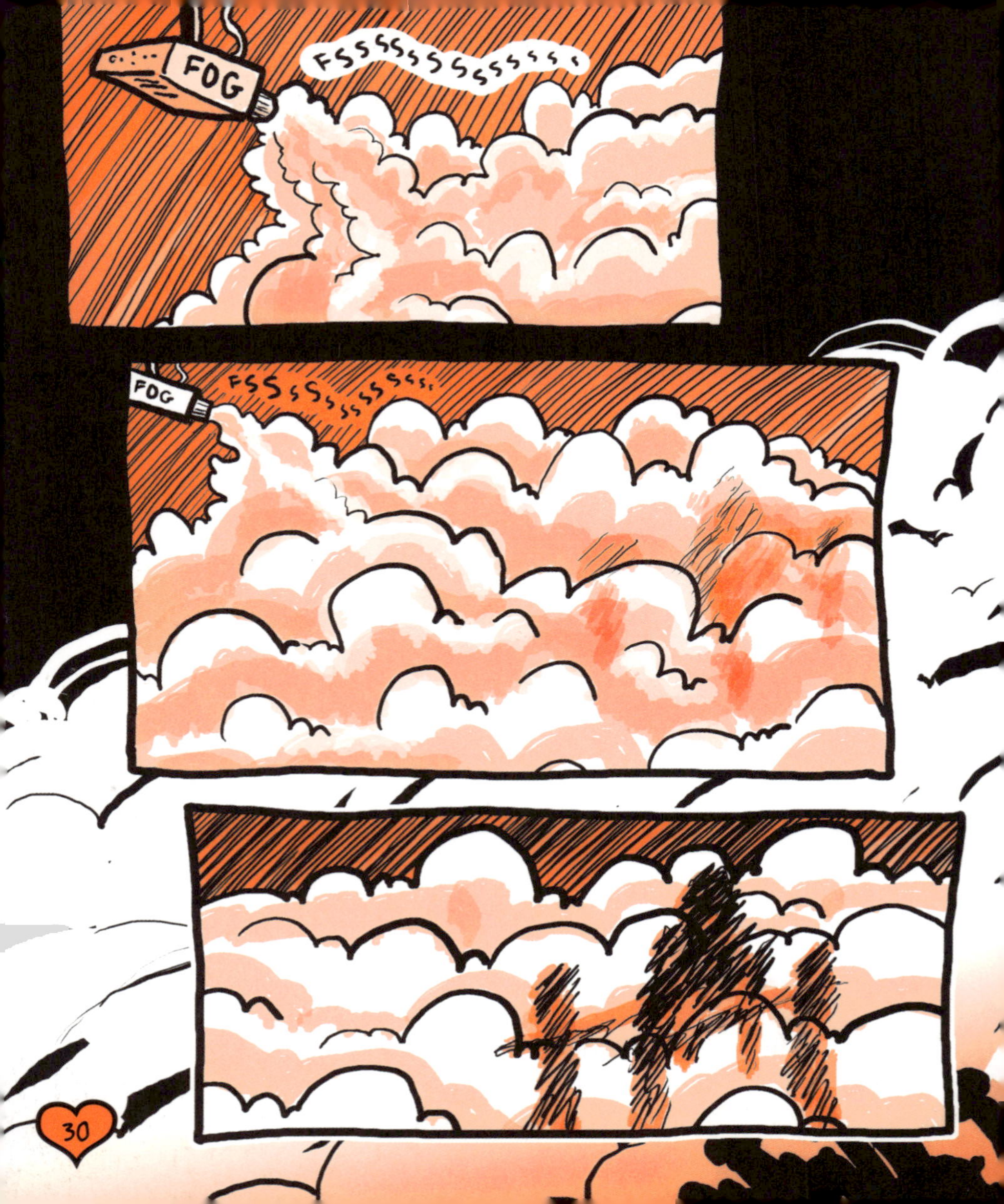

FOG
FSSSSSSSSSSSSSSS
FOG
FSSSSSSSSSSSS

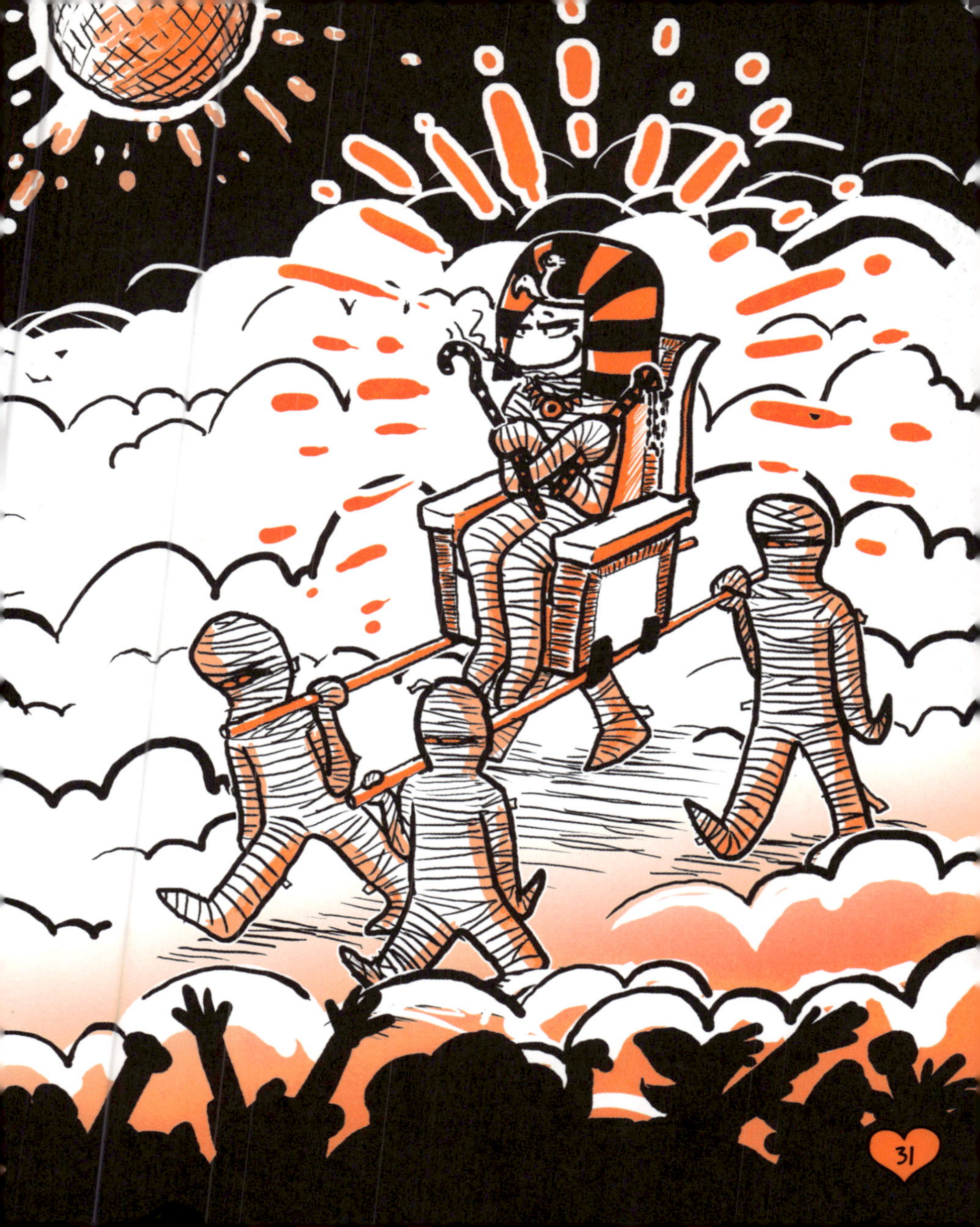

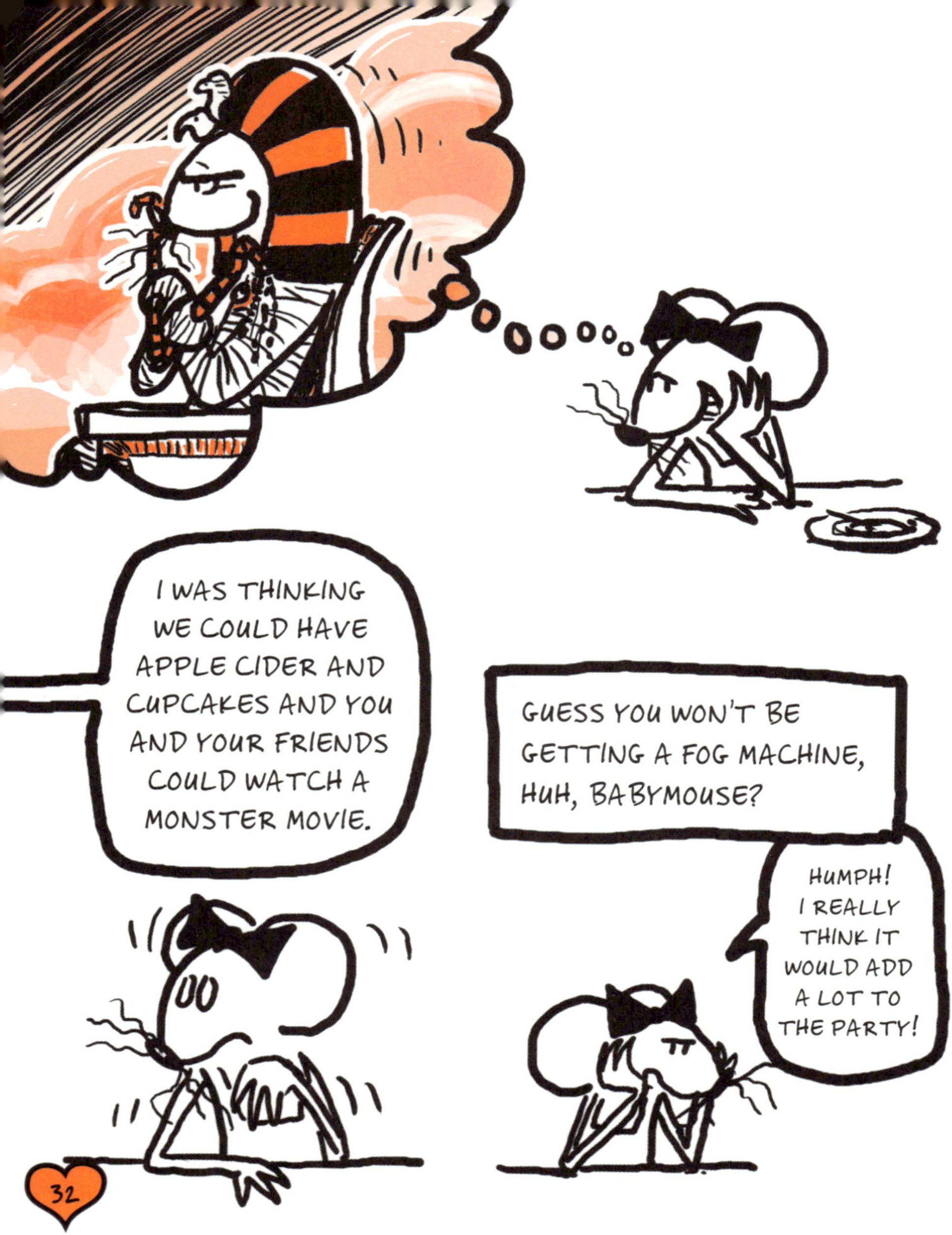
I WAS THINKING WE COULD HAVE APPLE CIDER AND CUPCAKES AND YOU AND YOUR FRIENDS COULD WATCH A MONSTER MOVIE.
GUESS YOU WON'T BE GETTING A FOG MACHINE, HUH, BABYMOUSE?
HUMPH! I REALLY THINK IT WOULD ADD A LOT TO THE PARTY!

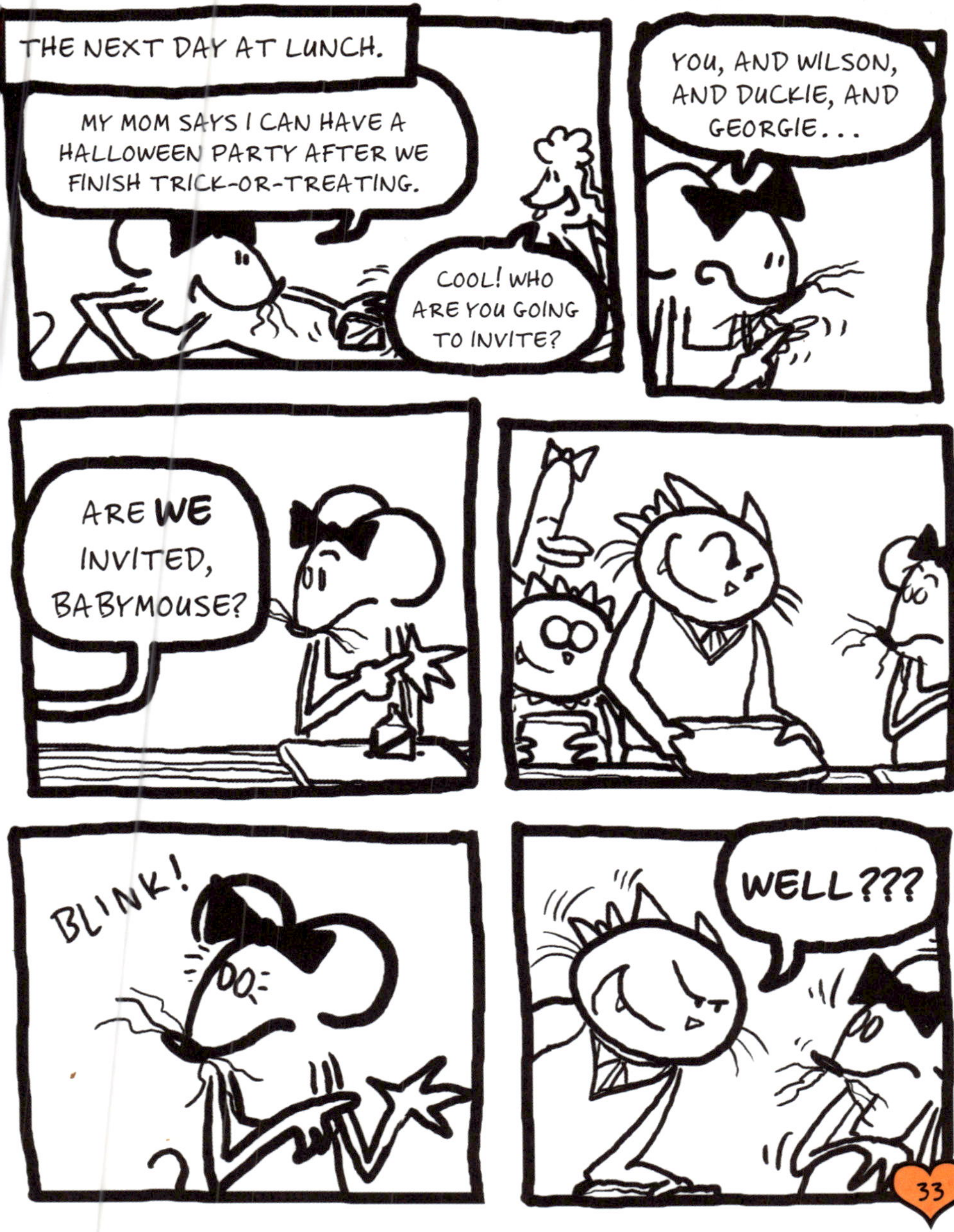
THE NEXT DAY AT LUNCH.
MY MOM SAYS I CAN HAVE A HALLOWEEN PARTY AFTER WE FINISH TRICK-OR-TREATING.
COOL! WHO ARE YOU GOING TO INVITE?
YOU, AND WILSON, AND DUCKIE, AND GEORGIE...
ARE **WE** INVITED, BABYMOUSE?
BLINK!
WELL???

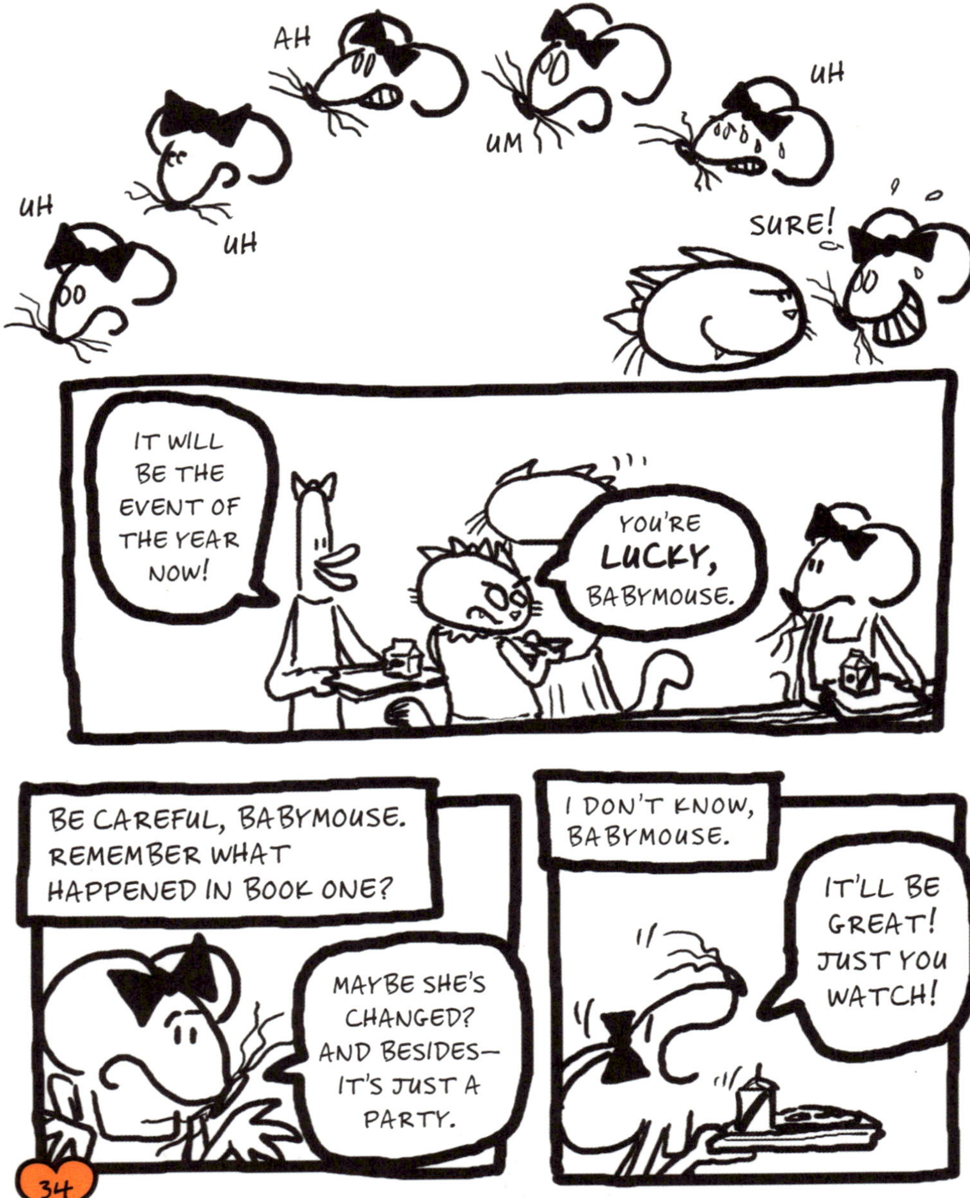
UH
UH
AH
UM
UH
SURE!
IT WILL BE THE EVENT OF THE YEAR NOW!
YOU'RE **LUCKY,** BABYMOUSE.
BE CAREFUL, BABYMOUSE. REMEMBER WHAT HAPPENED IN BOOK ONE?
MAYBE SHE'S CHANGED? AND BESIDES— IT'S JUST A PARTY.
I DON'T KNOW, BABYMOUSE.
IT'LL BE GREAT! JUST YOU WATCH!

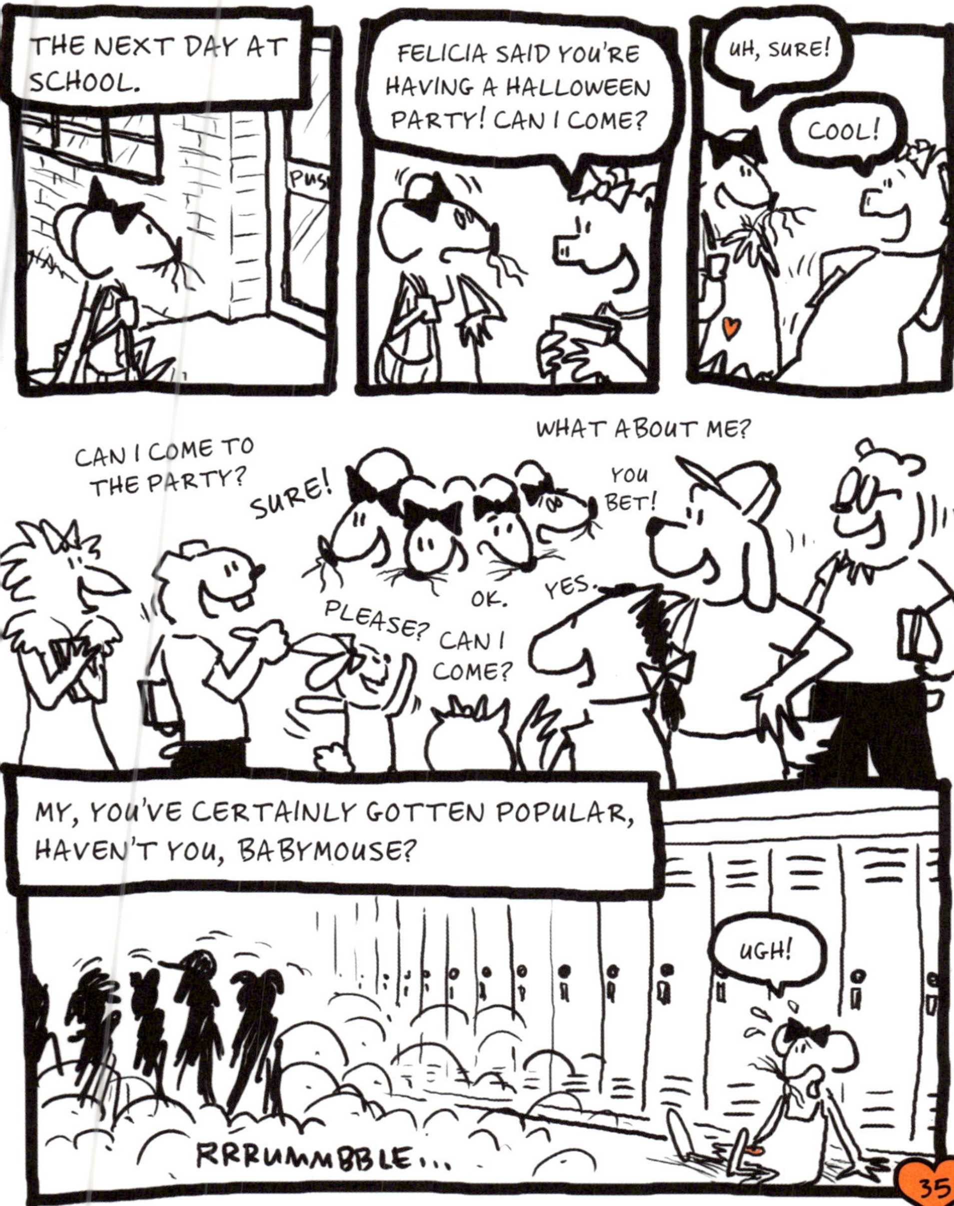
THE NEXT DAY AT SCHOOL.
PUSH
FELICIA SAID YOU'RE HAVING A HALLOWEEN PARTY! CAN I COME?
UH, SURE!
COOL!
CAN I COME TO THE PARTY?
SURE!
WHAT ABOUT ME?
YOU BET!
OK.
YES.
PLEASE?
CAN I COME?
MY, YOU'VE CERTAINLY GOTTEN POPULAR, HAVEN'T YOU, BABYMOUSE?
UGH!
RRRUMMBBLE...

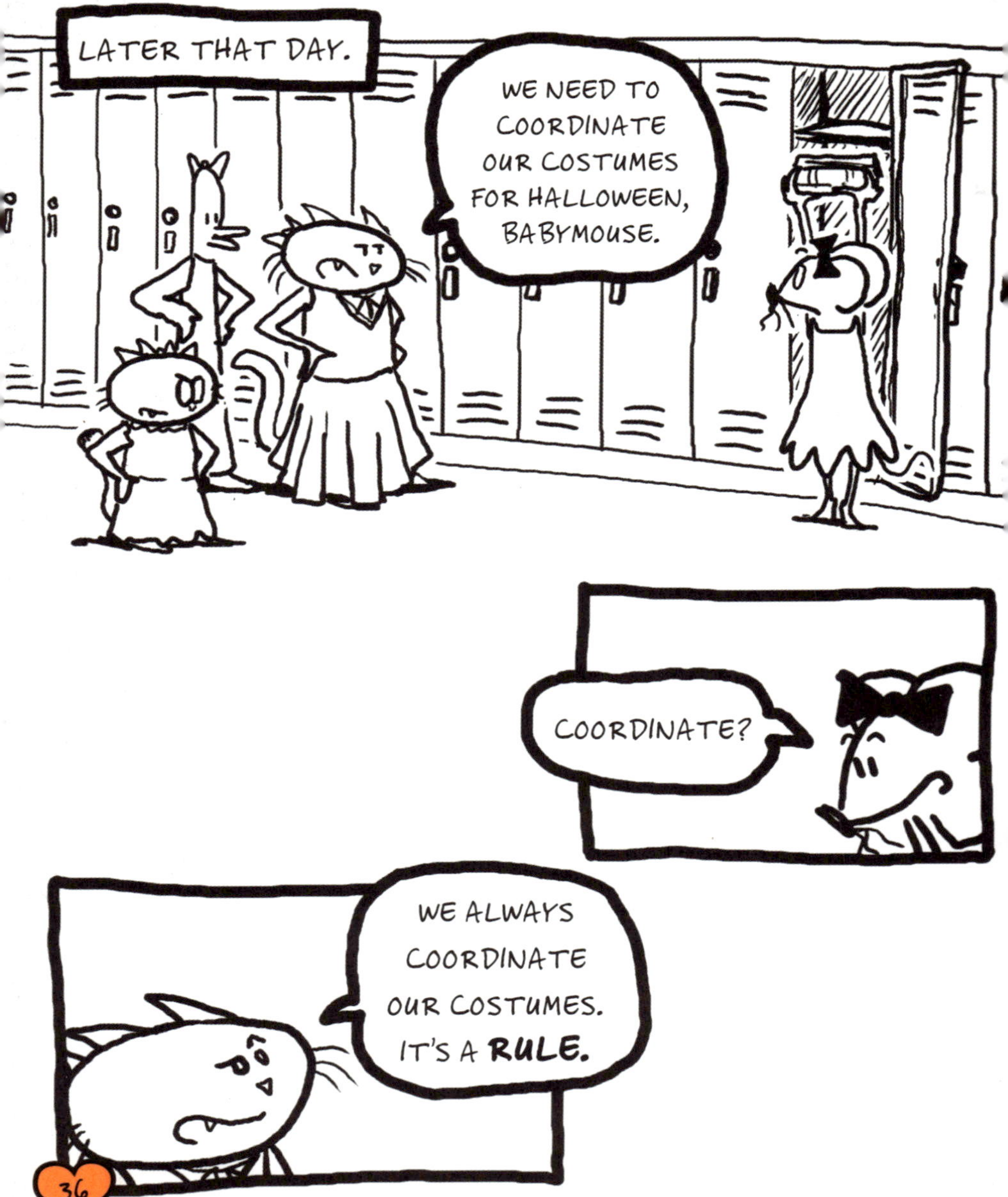
LATER THAT DAY.
WE NEED TO COORDINATE OUR COSTUMES FOR HALLOWEEN, BABYMOUSE.
COORDINATE?
WE ALWAYS COORDINATE OUR COSTUMES. IT'S A **RULE.**

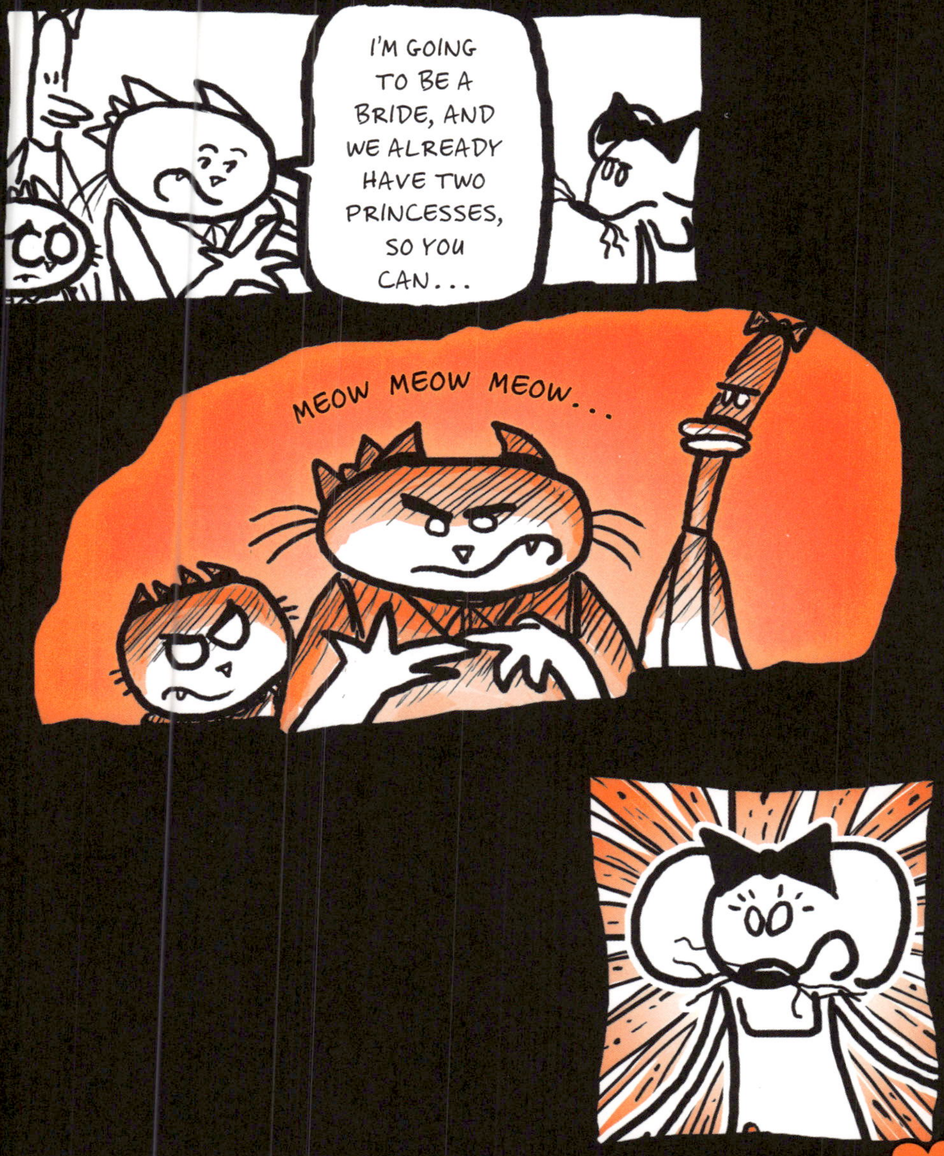
I'M GOING TO BE A BRIDE, AND WE ALREADY HAVE TWO PRINCESSES, SO YOU CAN...
MEOW MEOW MEOW...

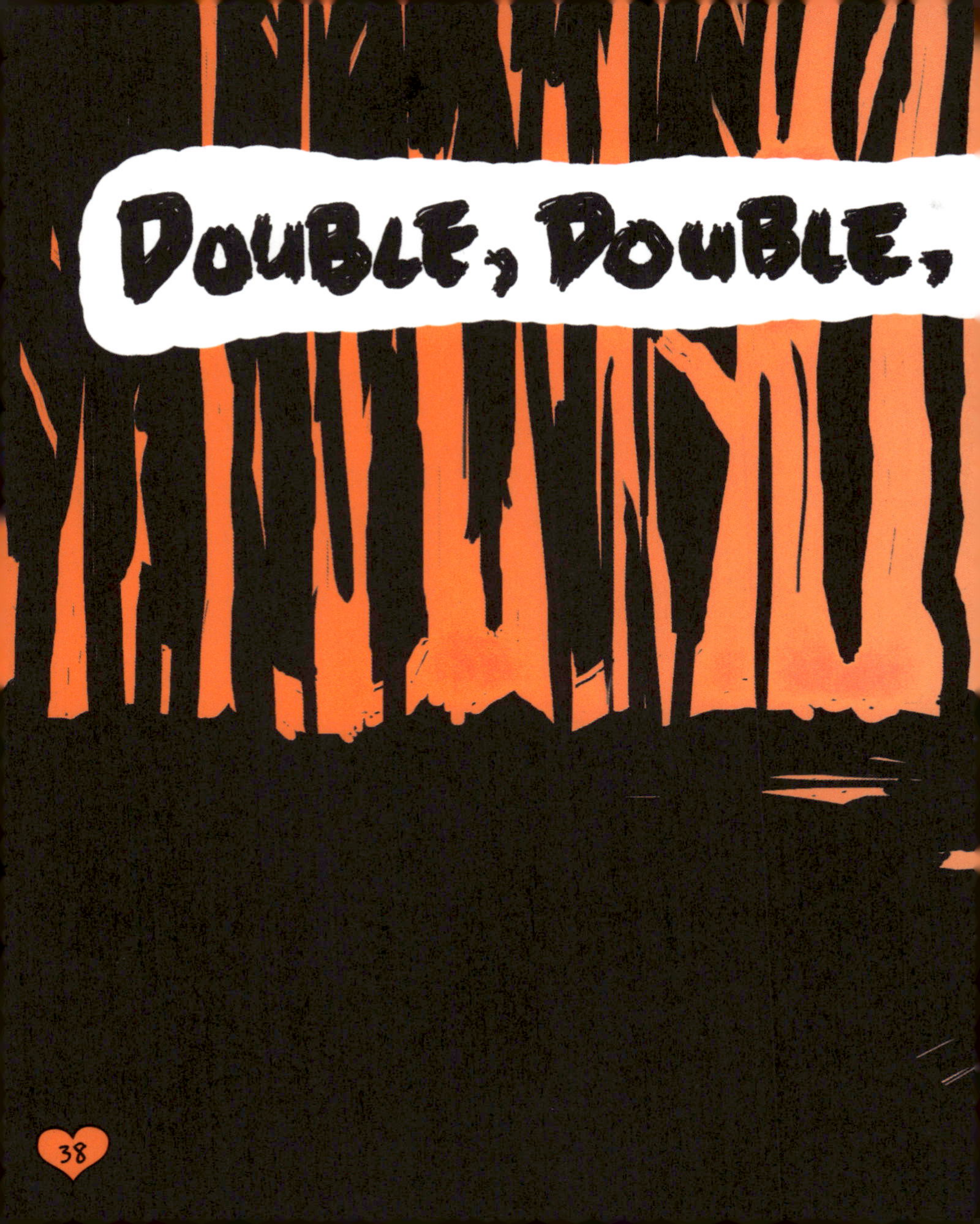
DOUBLE, DOUBLE,

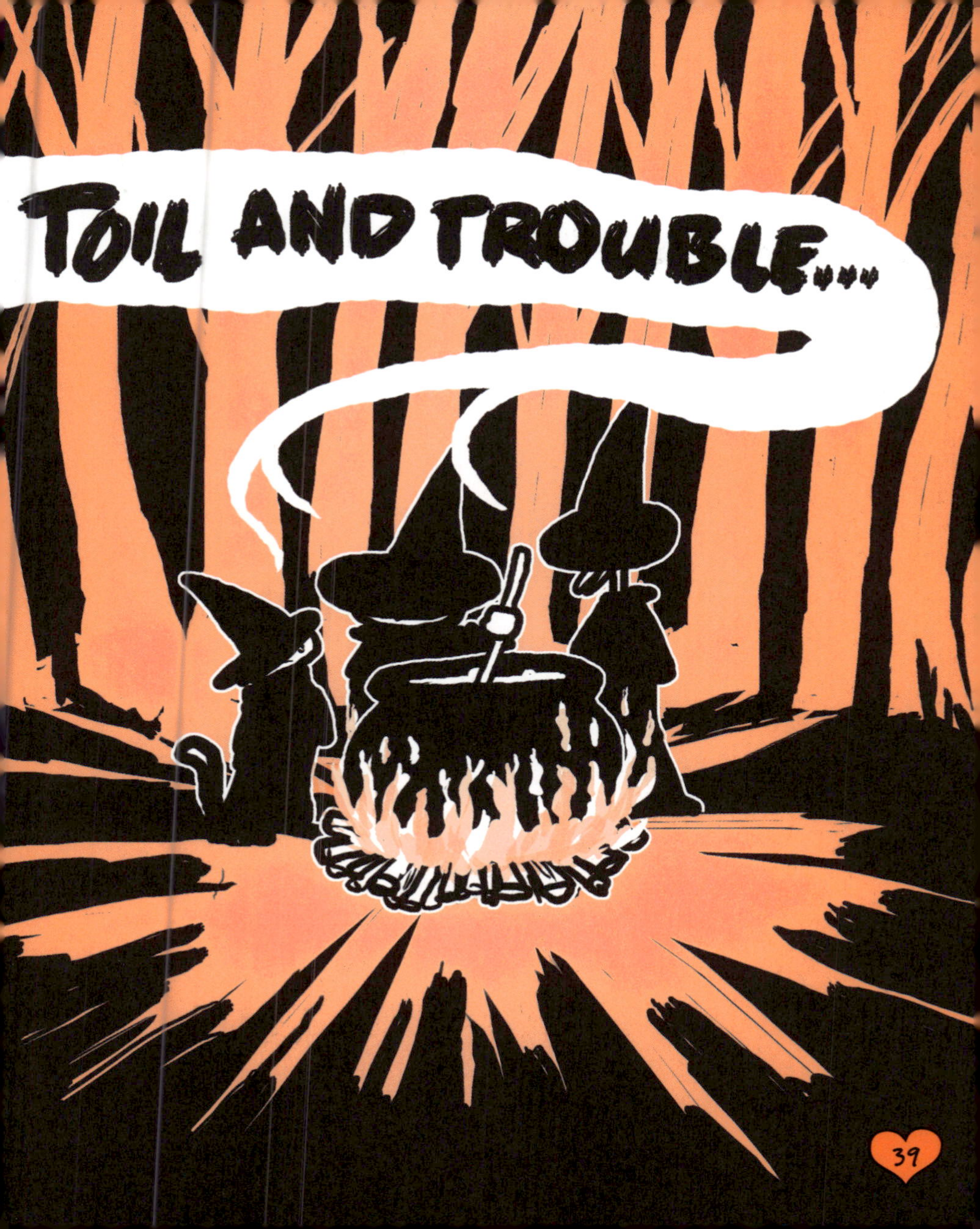
TOIL AND TROUBLE...

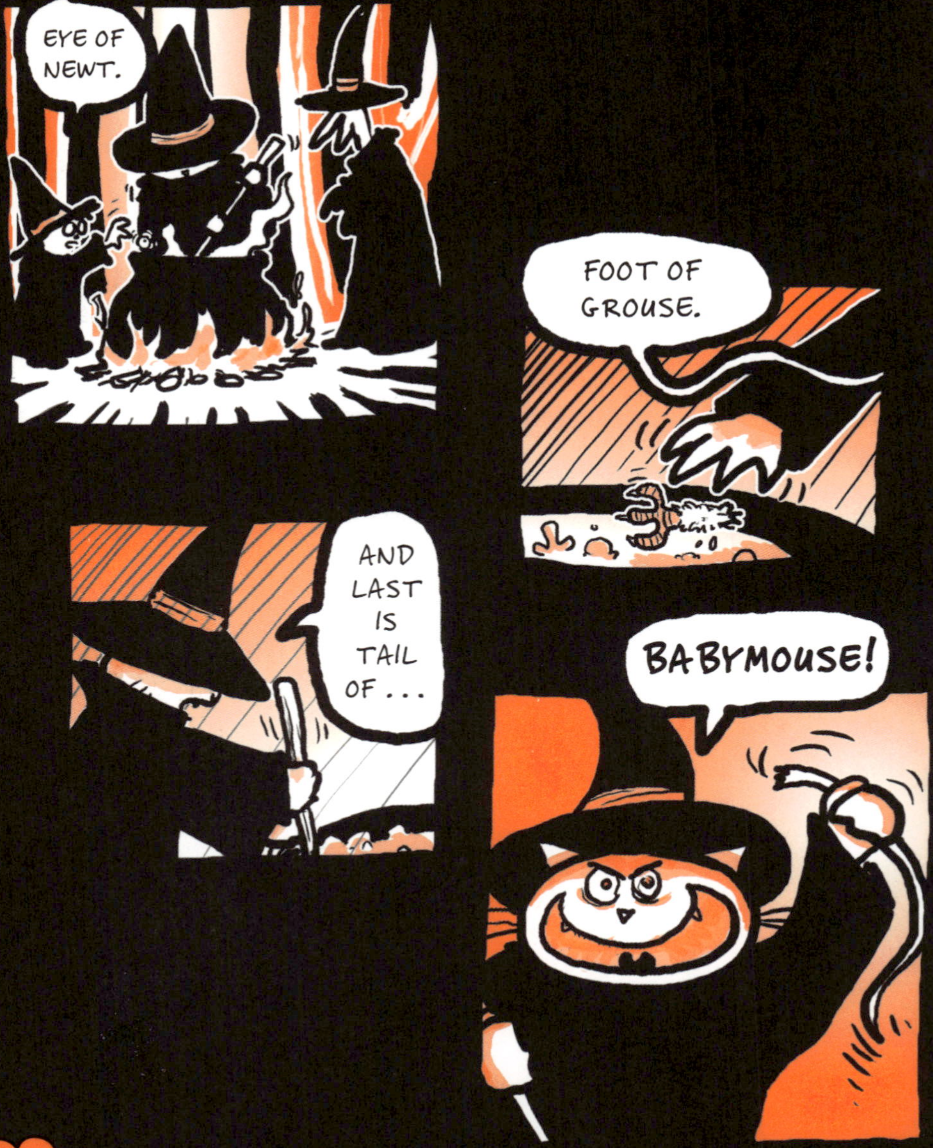
EYE OF NEWT.
FOOT OF GROUSE.
AND LAST IS TAIL OF . . .
BABYMOUSE!

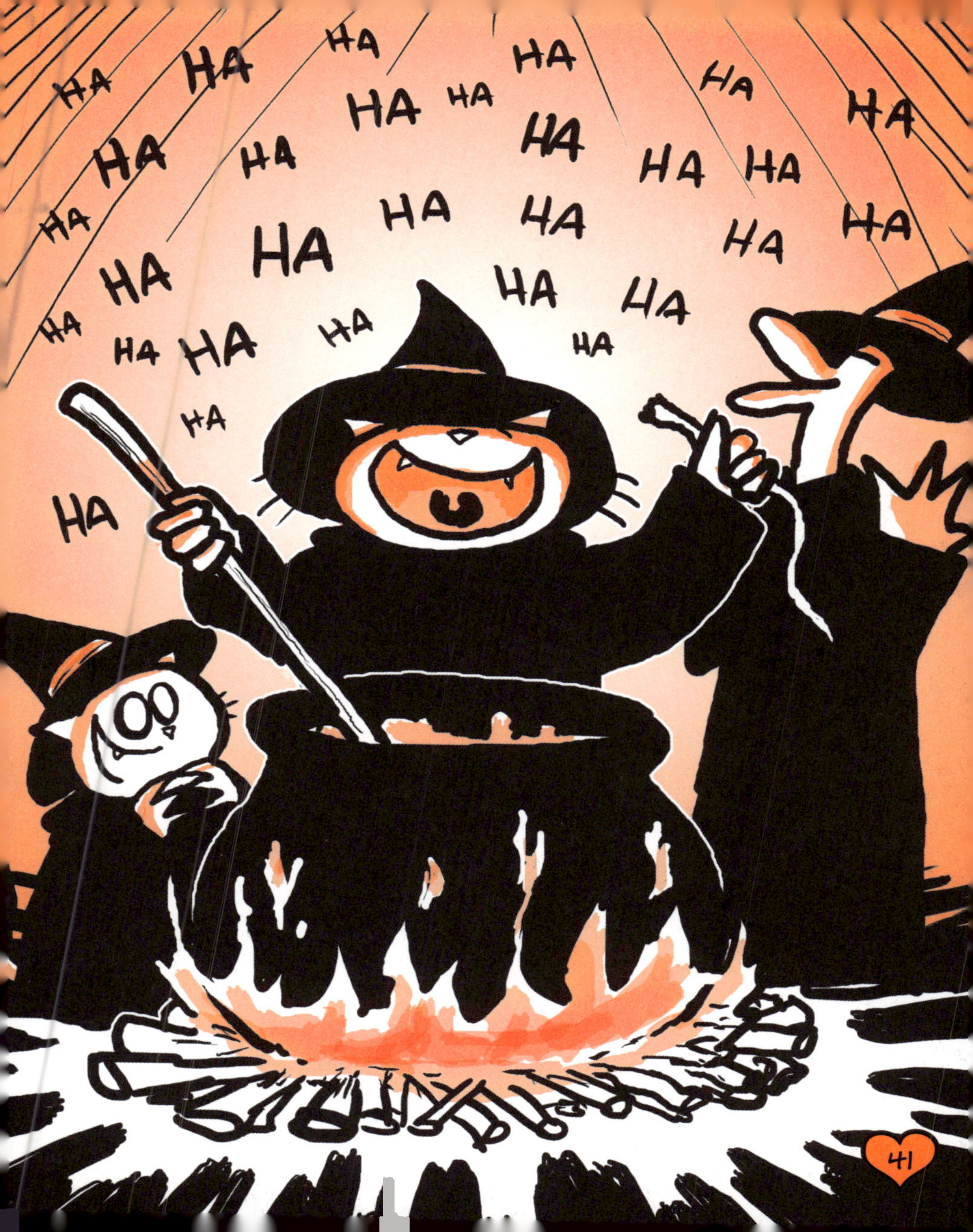
HA HA HA HA HA HA
HA HA HA
HA HA HA HA
HA HA HA HA HA
HA HA HA HA
HA HA HA HA
HA HA HA HA
HA
HA

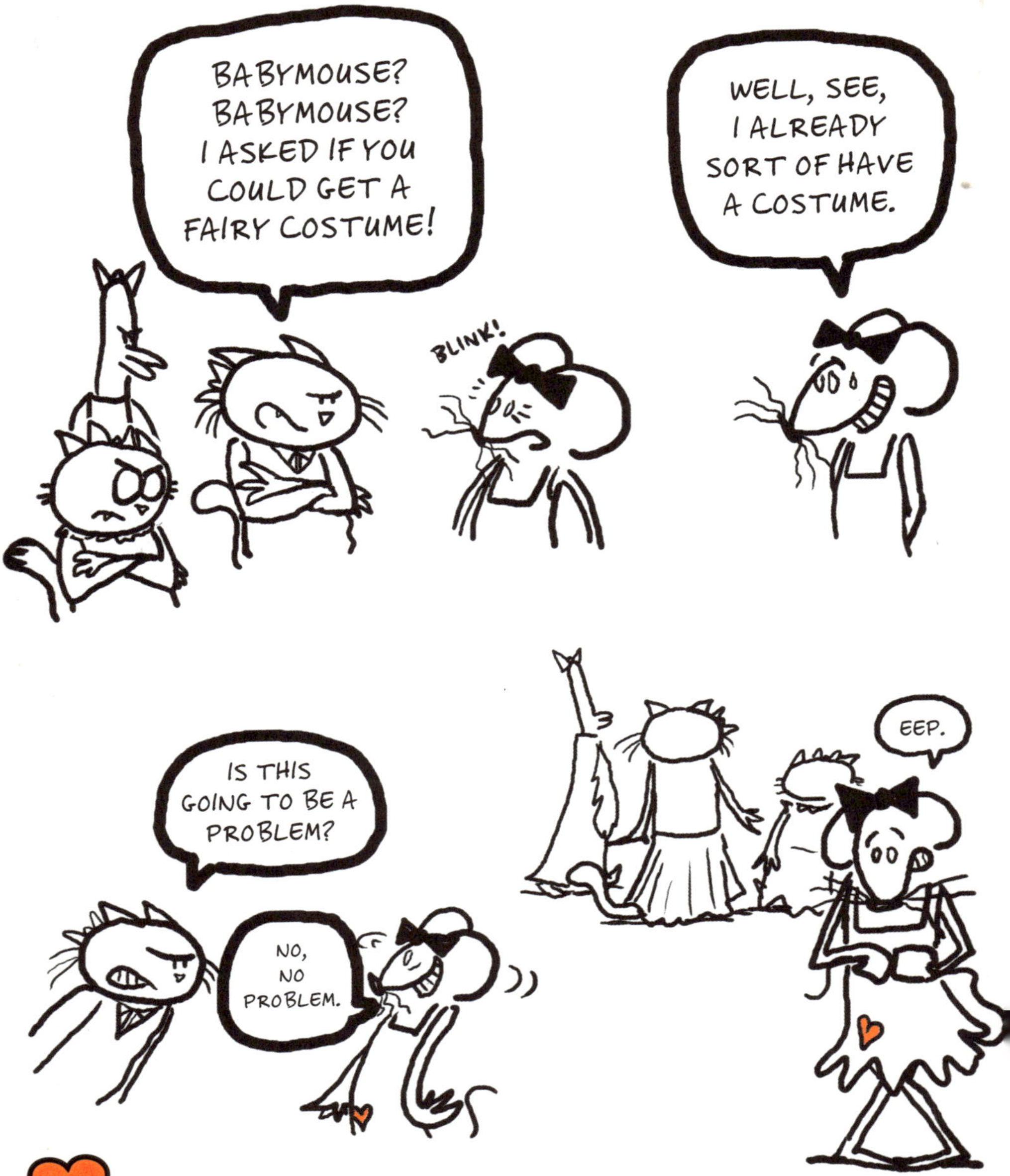
BABYMOUSE? BABYMOUSE? I ASKED IF YOU COULD GET A FAIRY COSTUME!
BLINK!
WELL, SEE, I ALREADY SORT OF HAVE A COSTUME.
IS THIS GOING TO BE A PROBLEM?
NO, NO PROBLEM.
EEP.

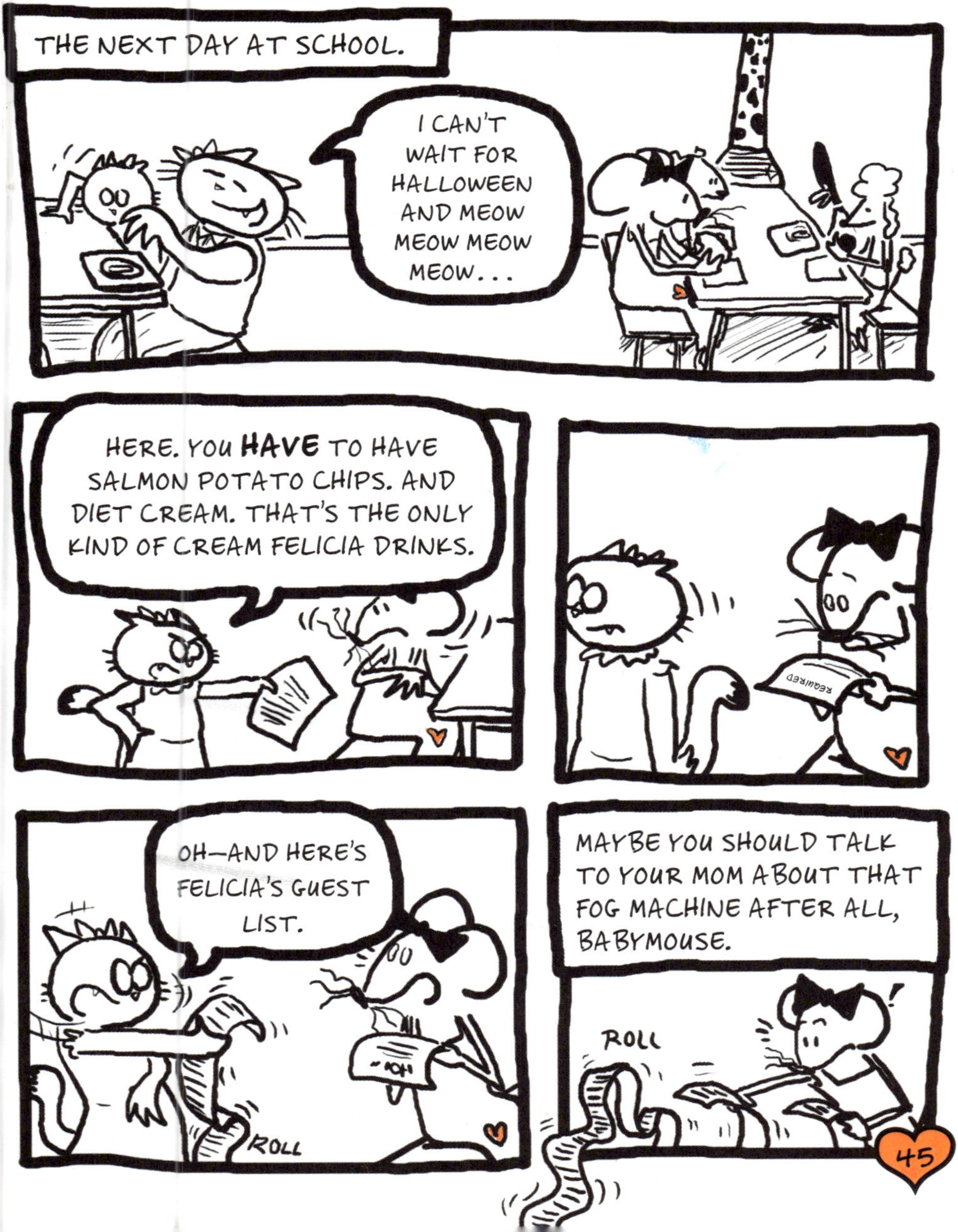
THE NEXT DAY AT SCHOOL.
I CAN'T WAIT FOR HALLOWEEN AND MEOW MEOW MEOW MEOW MEOW...
HERE. YOU **HAVE** TO HAVE SALMON POTATO CHIPS. AND DIET CREAM. THAT'S THE ONLY KIND OF CREAM FELICIA DRINKS.
REQUIRED
OH—AND HERE'S FELICIA'S GUEST LIST.
ROLL
MAYBE YOU SHOULD TALK TO YOUR MOM ABOUT THAT FOG MACHINE AFTER ALL, BABYMOUSE.
ROLL

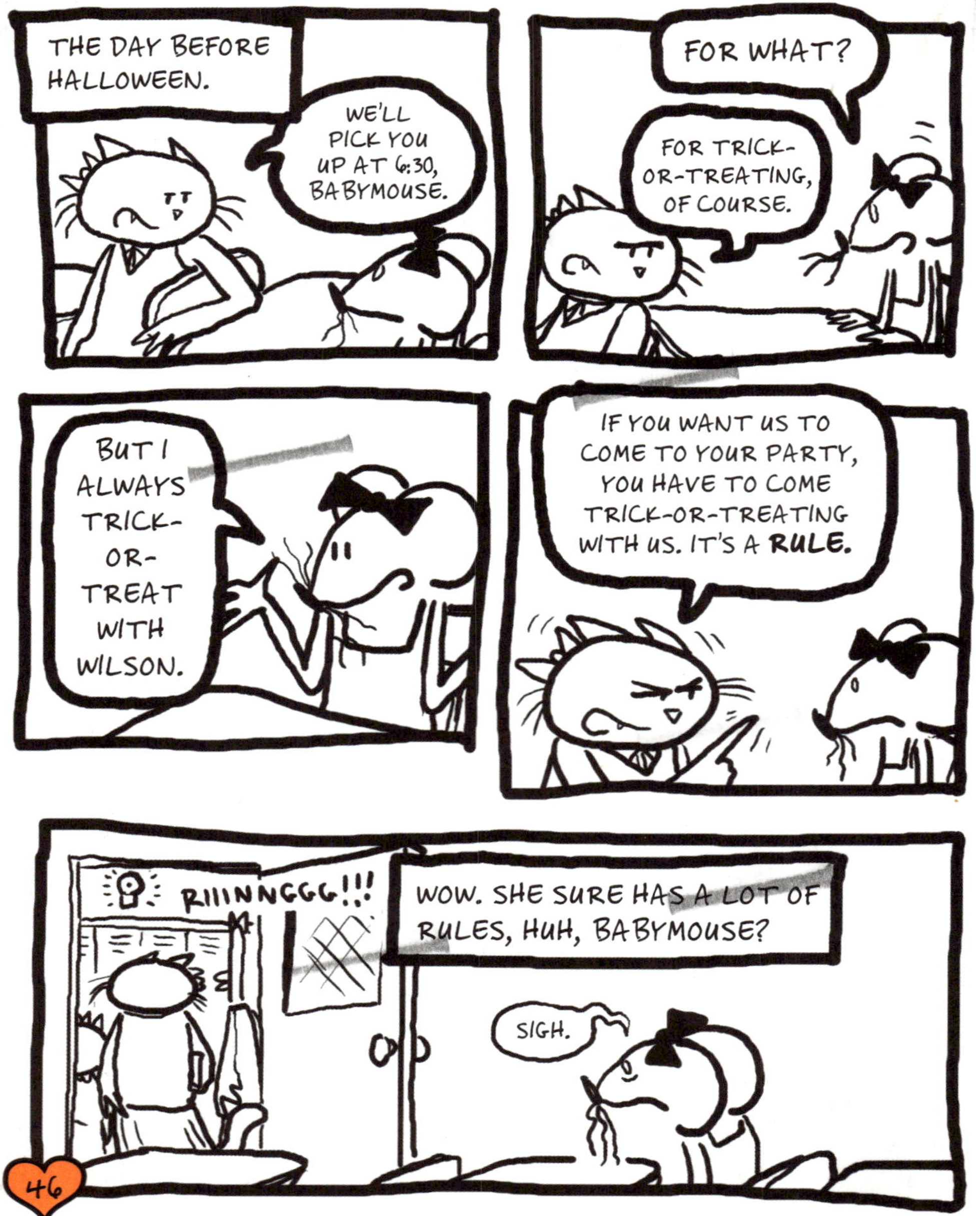
THE DAY BEFORE HALLOWEEN.
WE'LL PICK YOU UP AT 6:30, BABYMOUSE.
FOR WHAT?
FOR TRICK-OR-TREATING, OF COURSE.
BUT I ALWAYS TRICK-OR-TREAT WITH WILSON.
IF YOU WANT US TO COME TO YOUR PARTY, YOU HAVE TO COME TRICK-OR-TREATING WITH US. IT'S A **RULE.**
RIIINNGGG!!!
WOW. SHE SURE HAS A LOT OF RULES, HUH, BABYMOUSE?
SIGH.

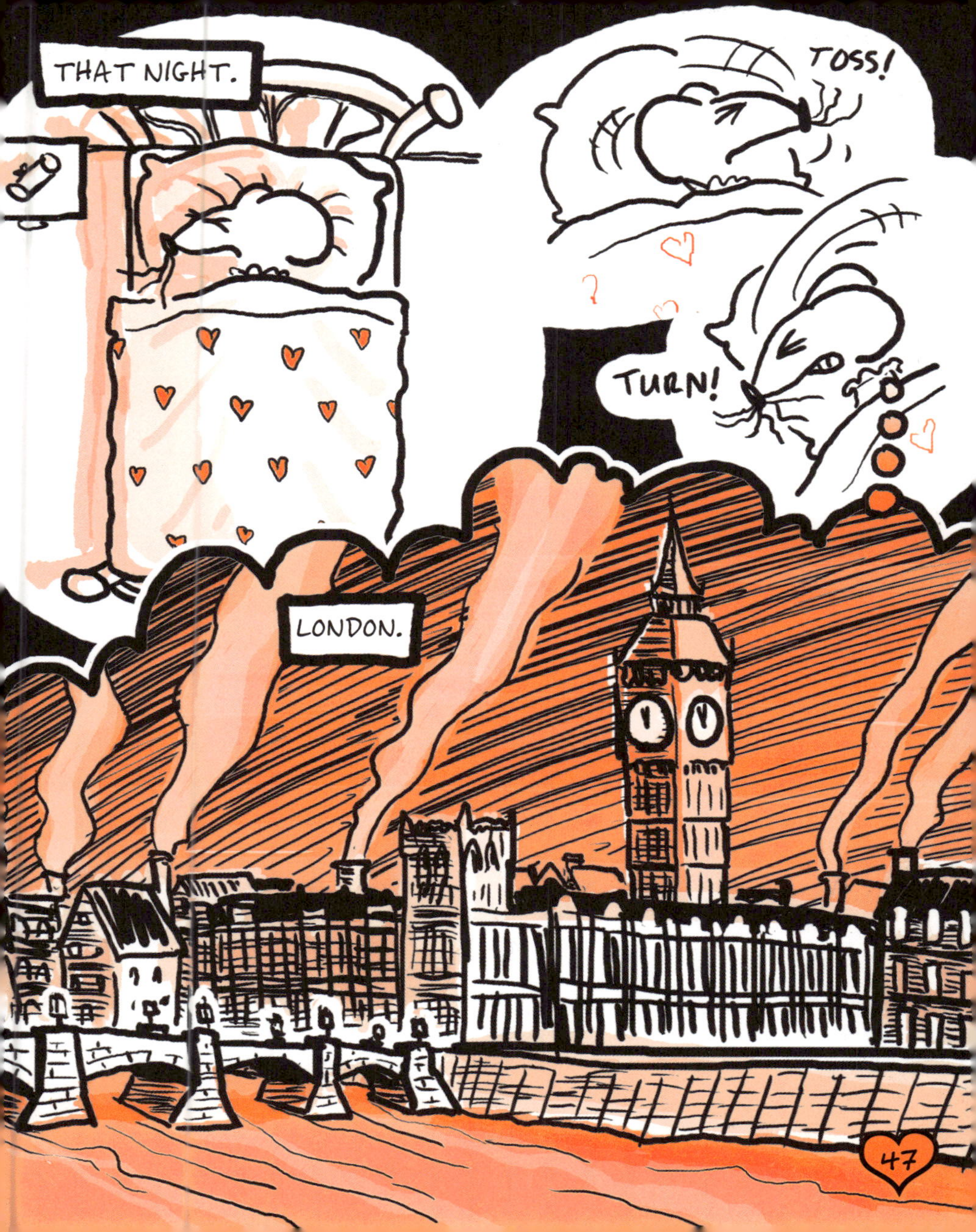
THAT NIGHT.
TOSS!
TURN!
LONDON.

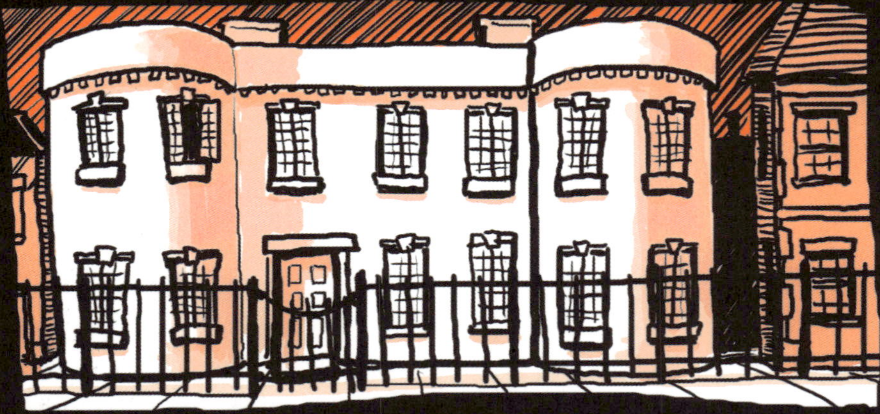

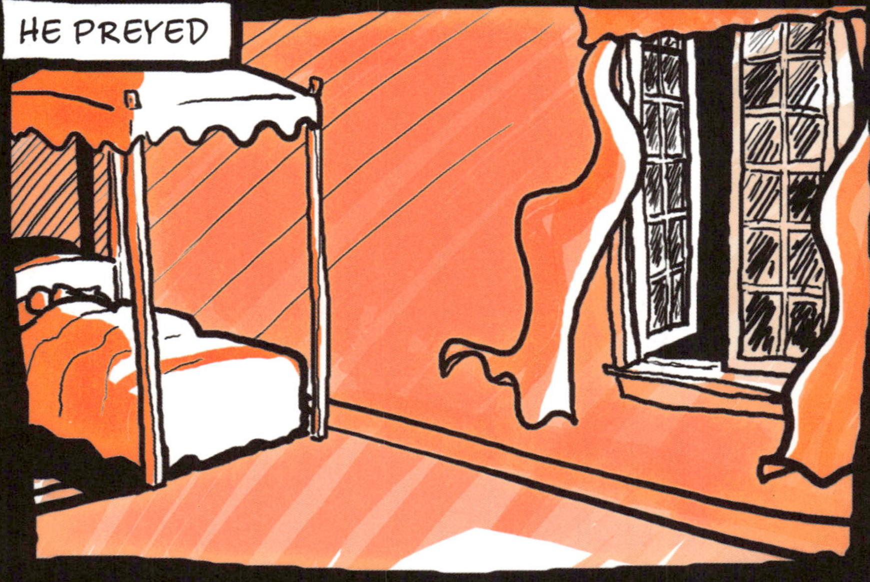
HE PREYED

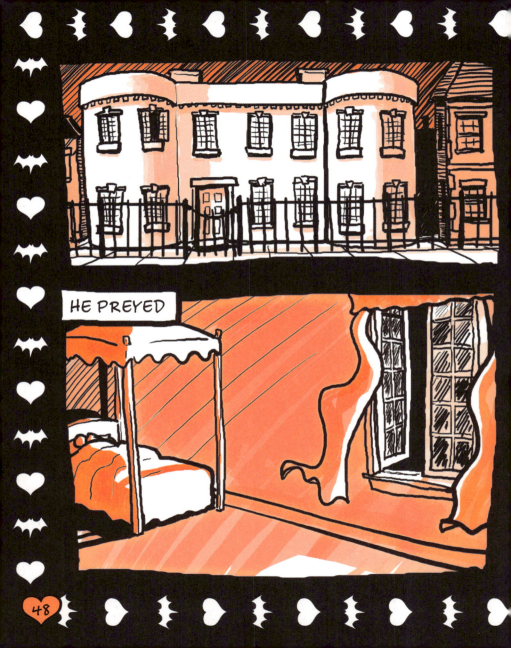

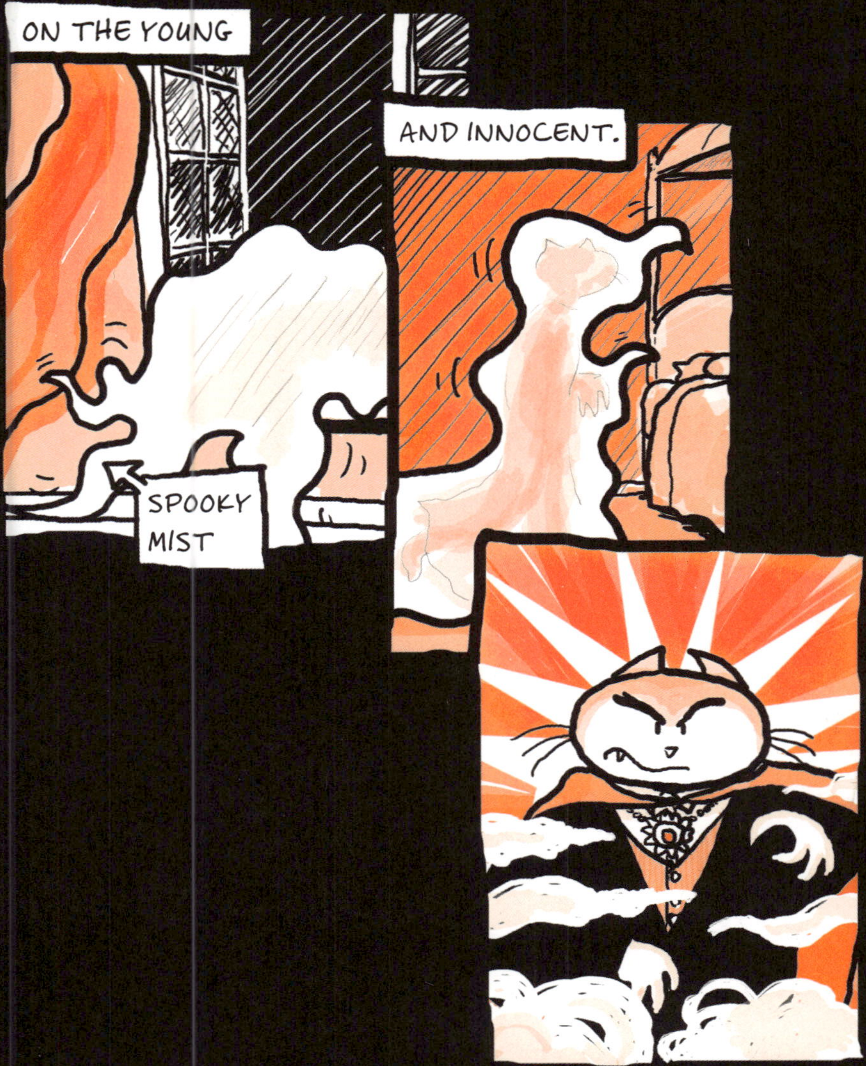
ON THE YOUNG
SPOOKY
MIST
AND INNOCENT.

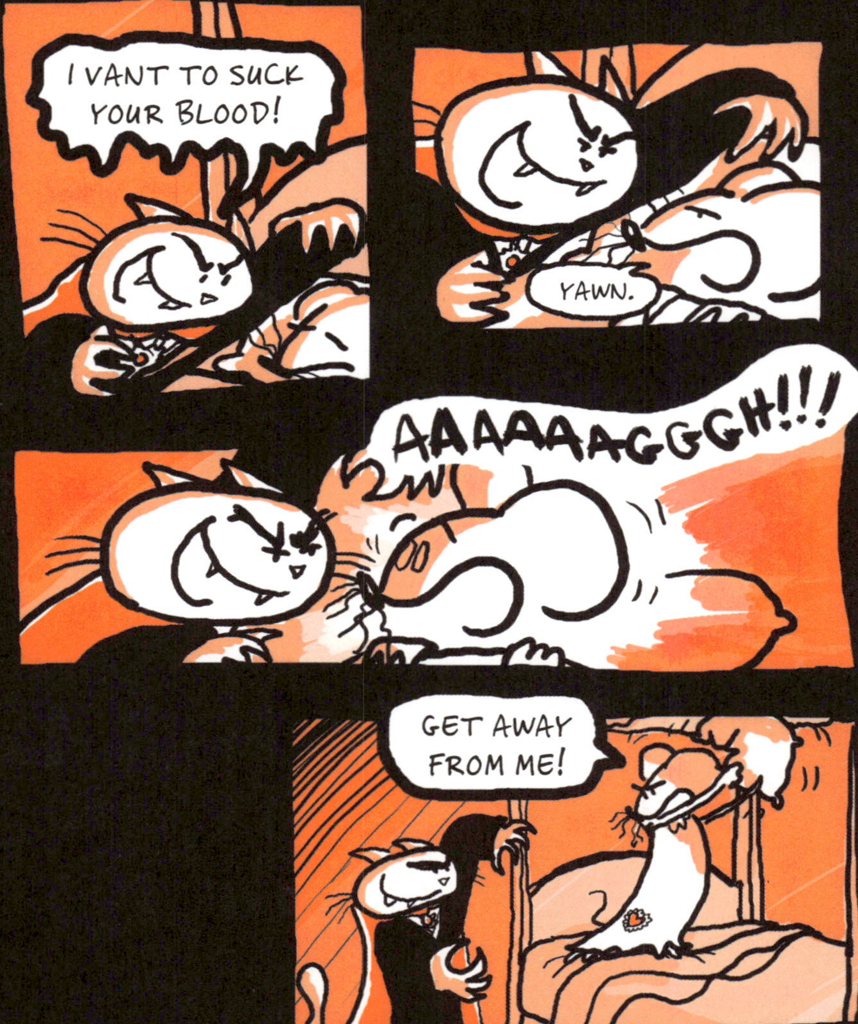
I VANT TO SUCK YOUR BLOOD!
YAWN.
AAAAAAGGGH!!!
GET AWAY FROM ME!

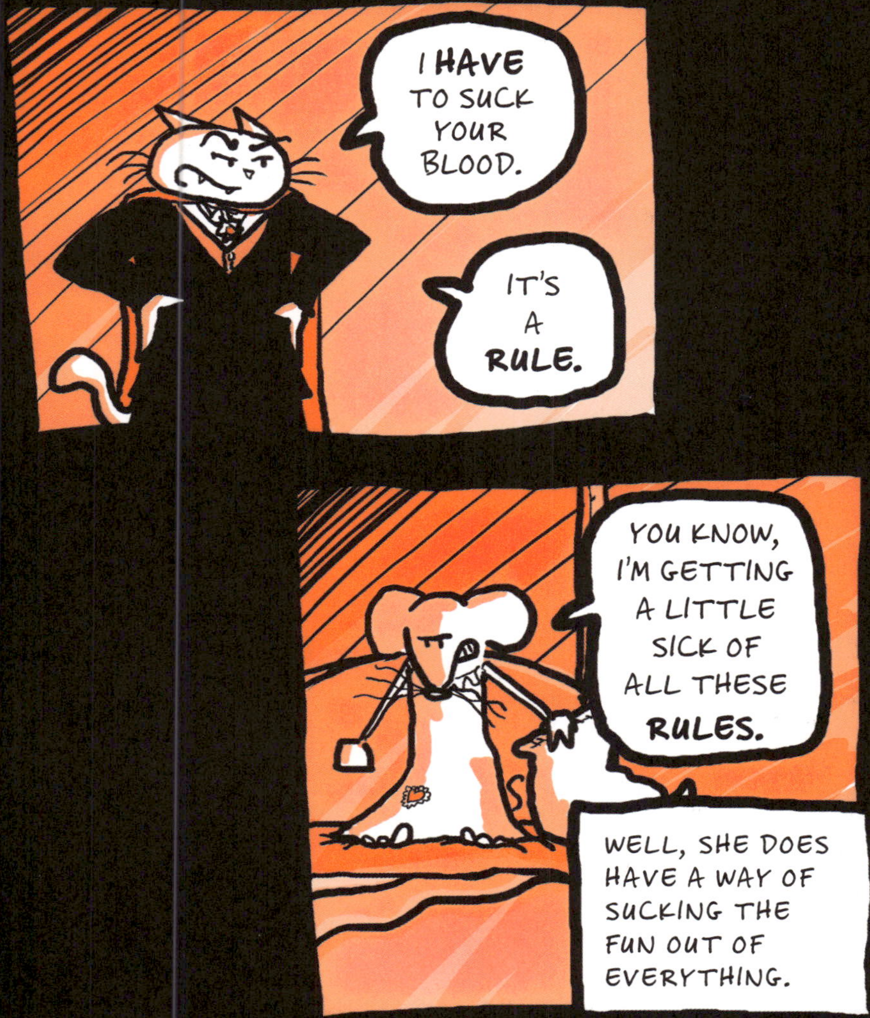
I HAVE TO SUCK YOUR BLOOD.
IT'S A RULE.
YOU KNOW, I'M GETTING A LITTLE SICK OF ALL THESE RULES.
WELL, SHE DOES HAVE A WAY OF SUCKING THE FUN OUT OF EVERYTHING.

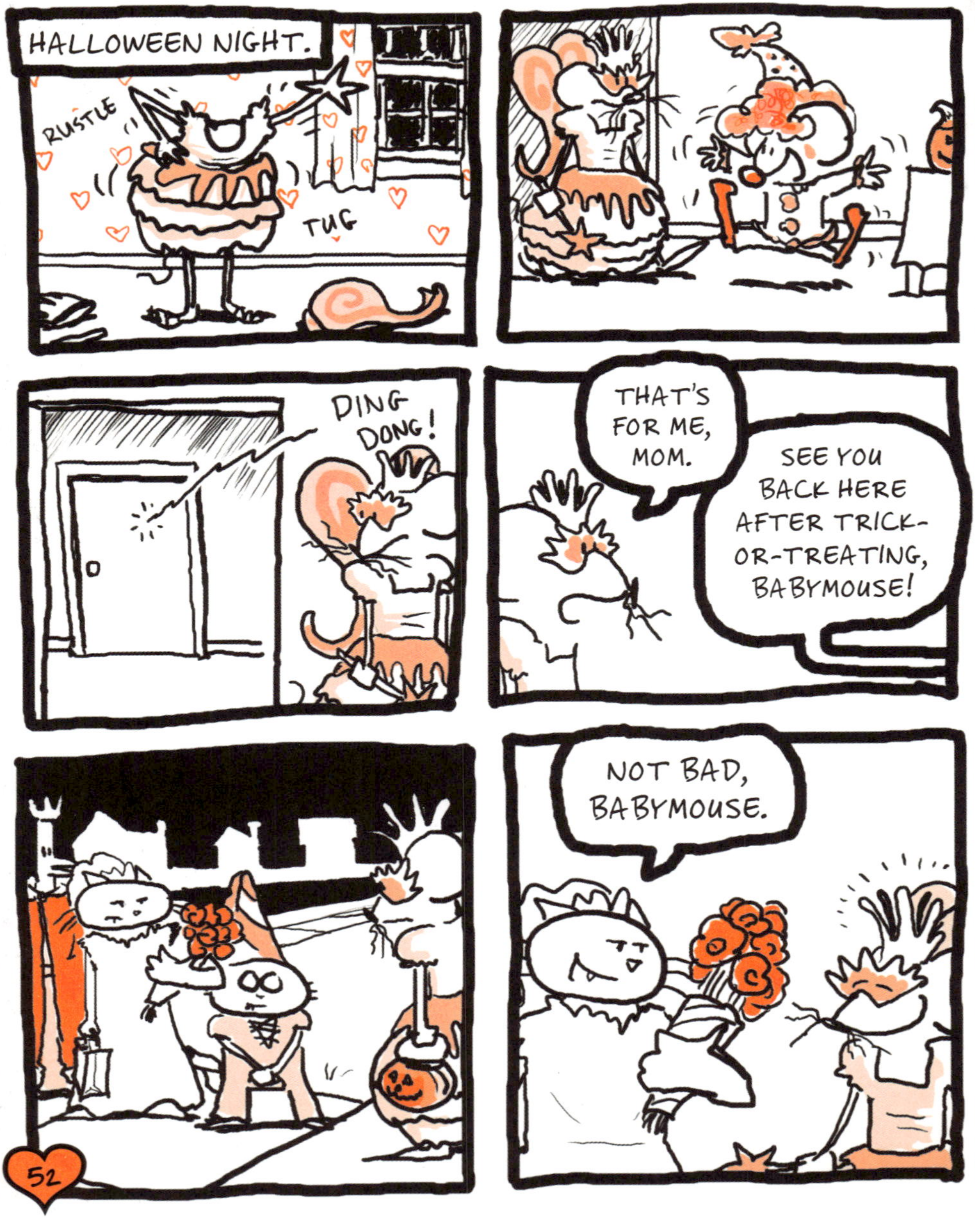
HALLOWEEN NIGHT.
RUSTLE
TUG
DING DONG!
THAT'S FOR ME, MOM.
SEE YOU BACK HERE AFTER TRICK-OR-TREATING, BABYMOUSE!
NOT BAD, BABYMOUSE.

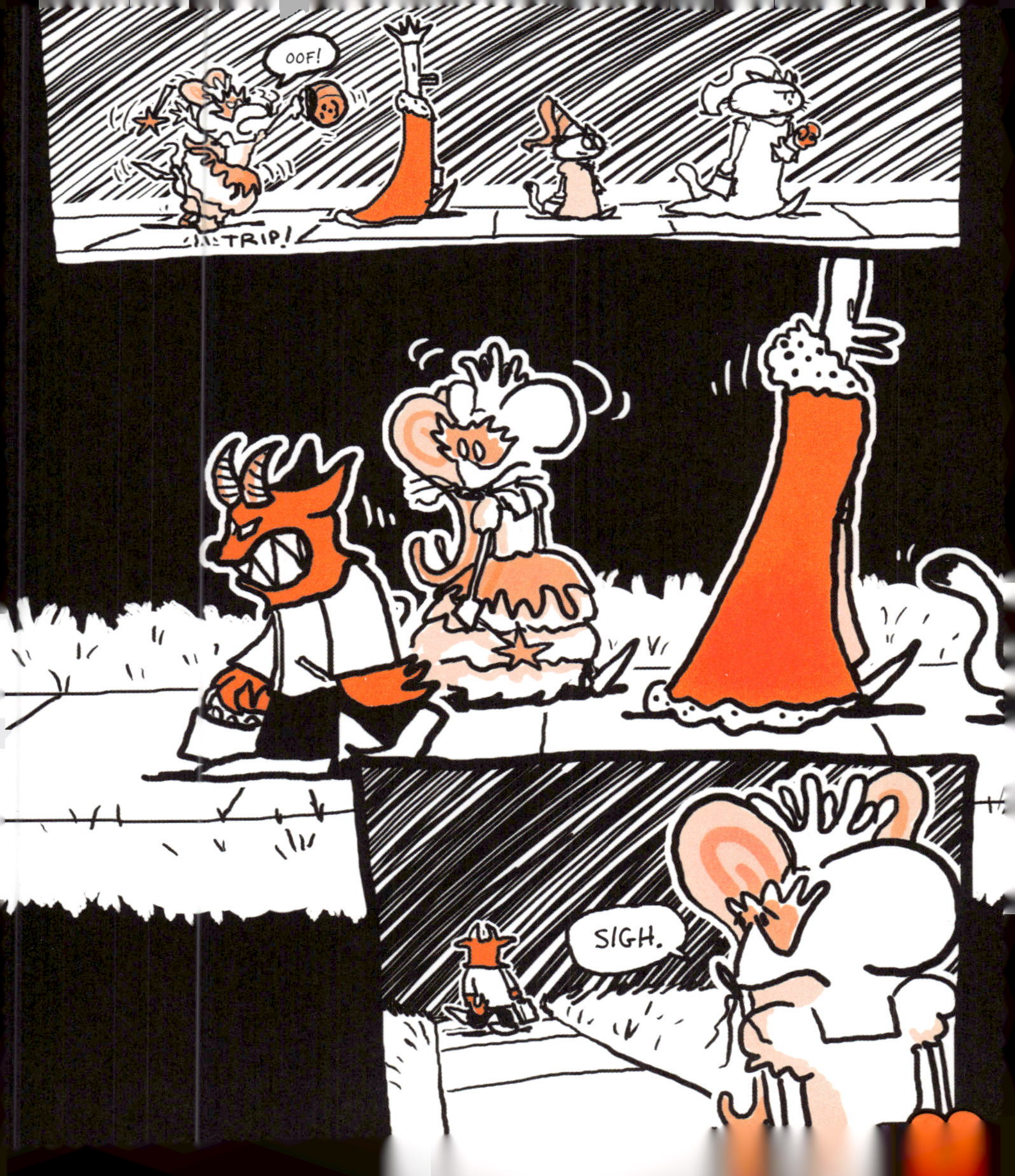
OOF!
TRIP!
SIGH.

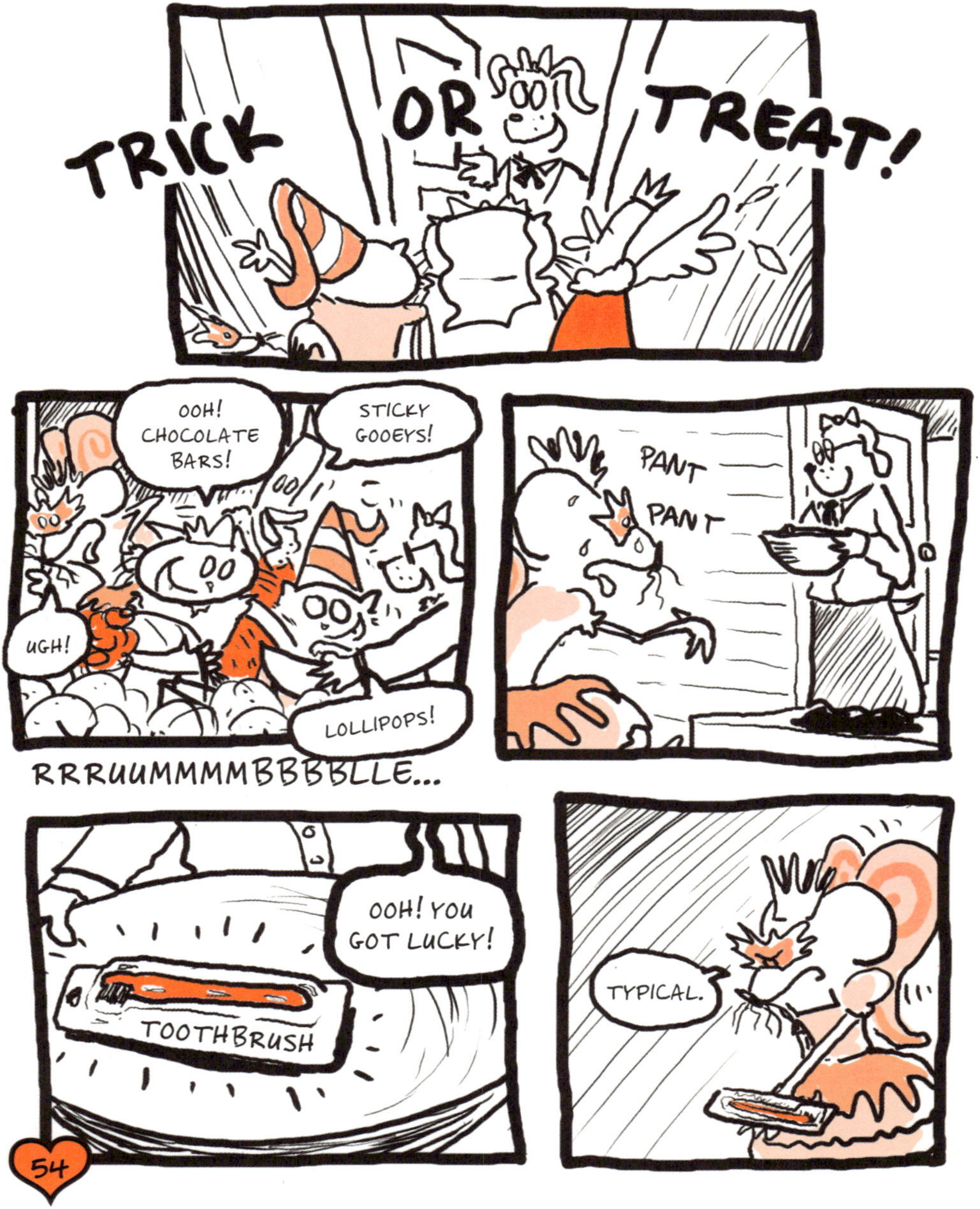
TRICK OR TREAT!
OOH! CHOCOLATE BARS!
STICKY GOOEYS!
UGH!
LOLLIPOPS!
PANT PANT
RRRUUMMMMBBBBLLE...
OOH! YOU GOT LUCKY!
TOOTHBRUSH
TYPICAL.

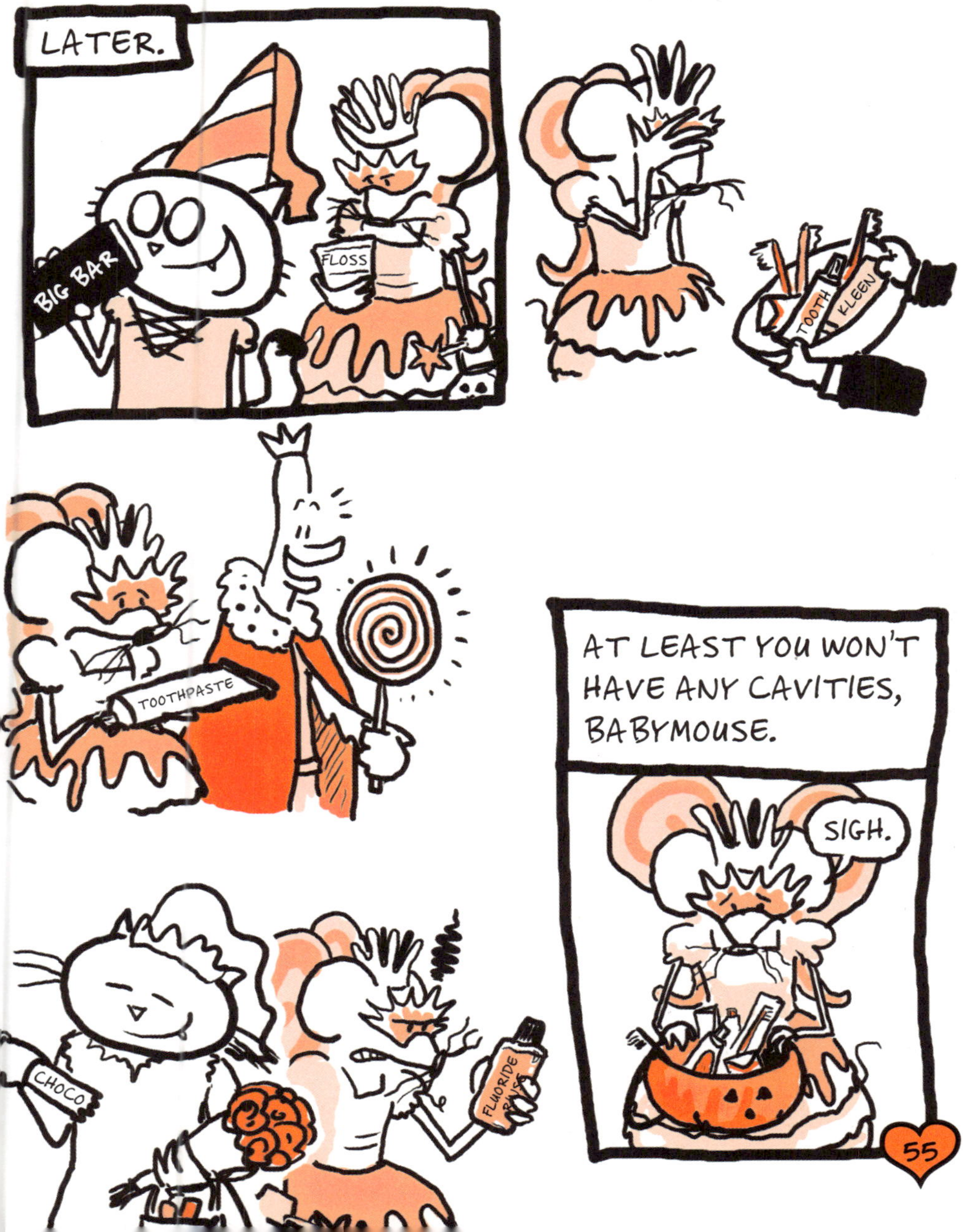
LATER.
BIG BAR
FLOSS
TOOTH
KLEEN
TOOTHPASTE
CHOCO
FLUORIDE RINSE
AT LEAST YOU WON'T HAVE ANY CAVITIES, BABYMOUSE.
SIGH.

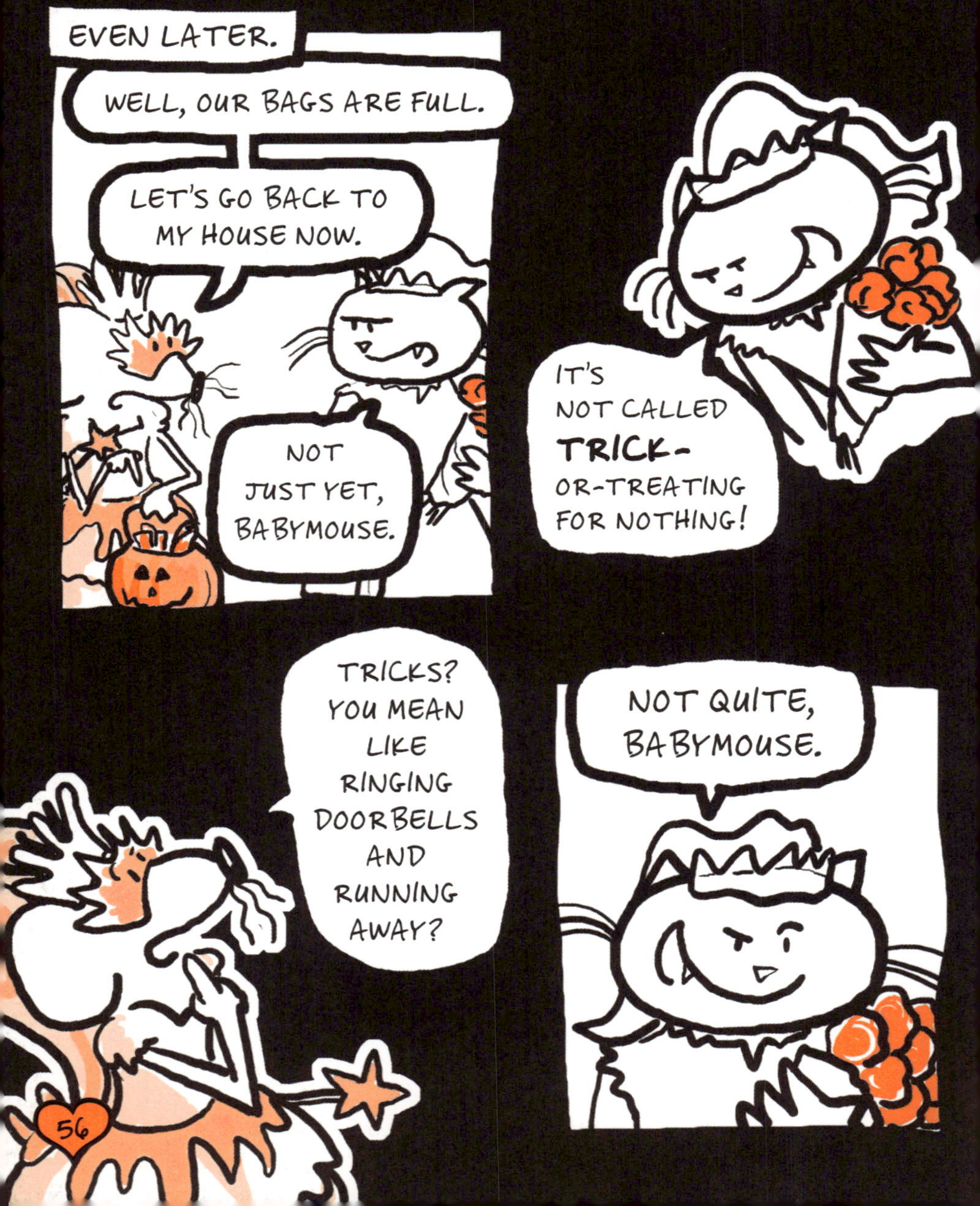
EVEN LATER.
WELL, OUR BAGS ARE FULL.
LET'S GO BACK TO MY HOUSE NOW.
NOT JUST YET, BABYMOUSE.
IT'S NOT CALLED **TRICK-** OR-TREATING FOR NOTHING!
TRICKS? YOU MEAN LIKE RINGING DOORBELLS AND RUNNING AWAY?
NOT QUITE, BABYMOUSE.

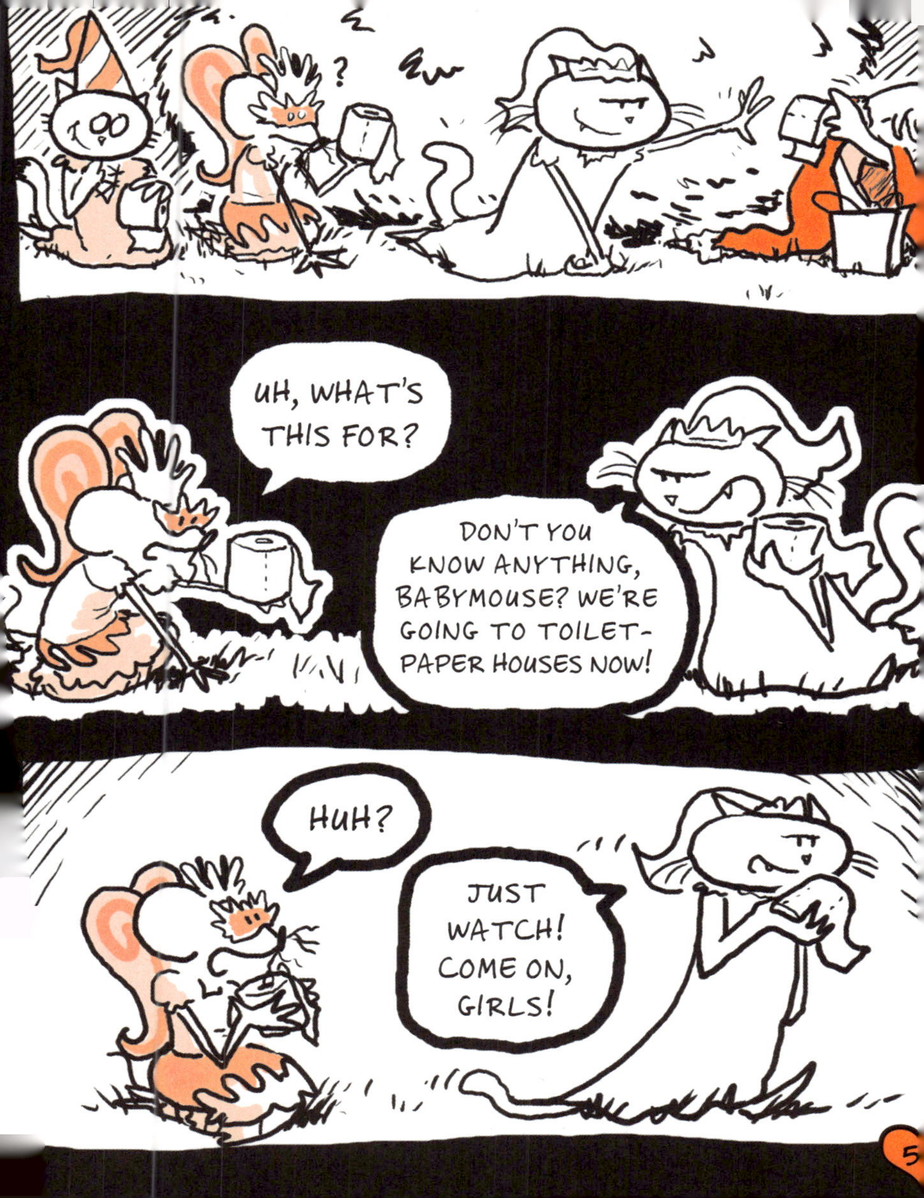
?
UH, WHAT'S THIS FOR?
DON'T YOU KNOW ANYTHING, BABYMOUSE? WE'RE GOING TO TOILET-PAPER HOUSES NOW!
HUH?
JUST WATCH! COME ON, GIRLS!

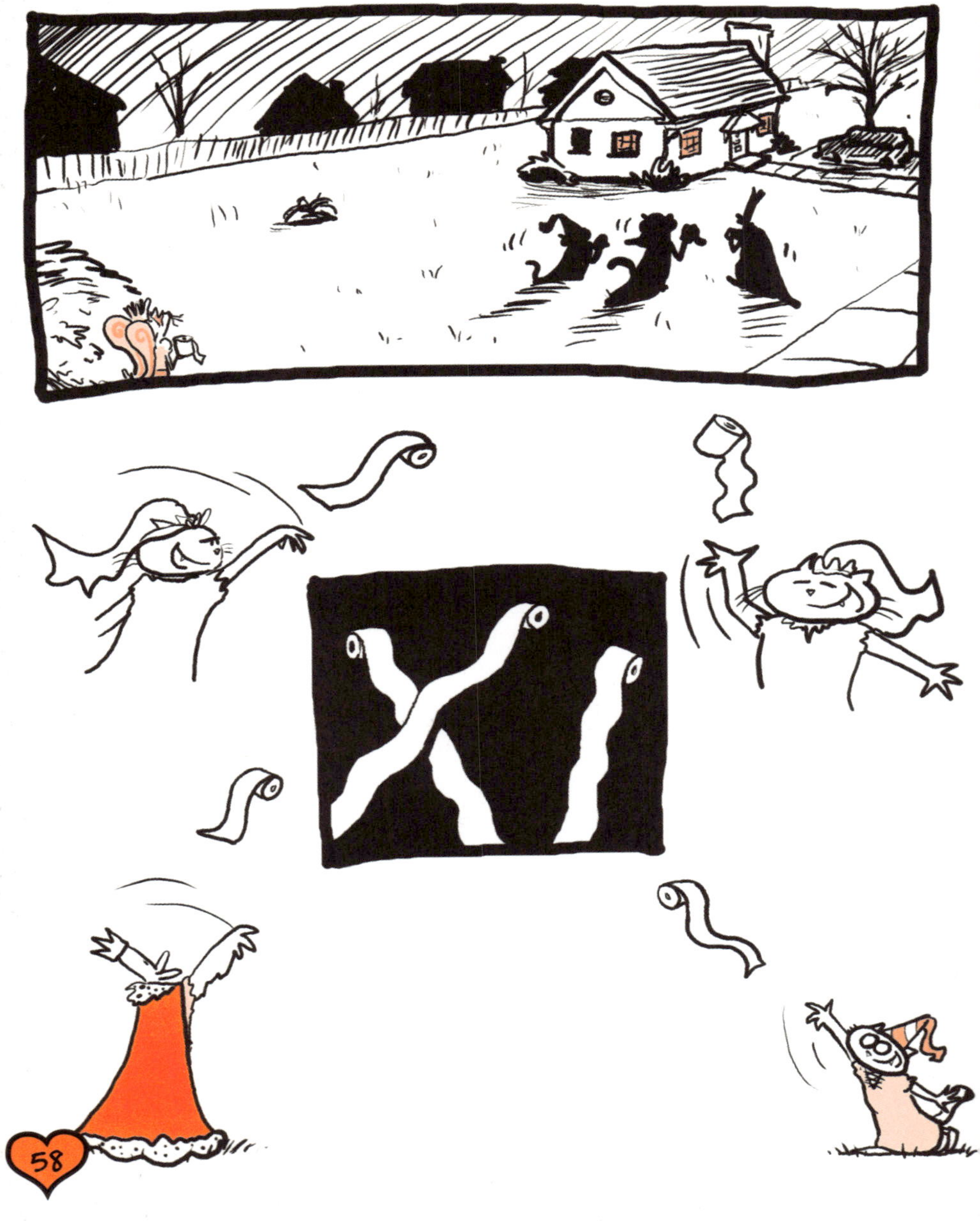

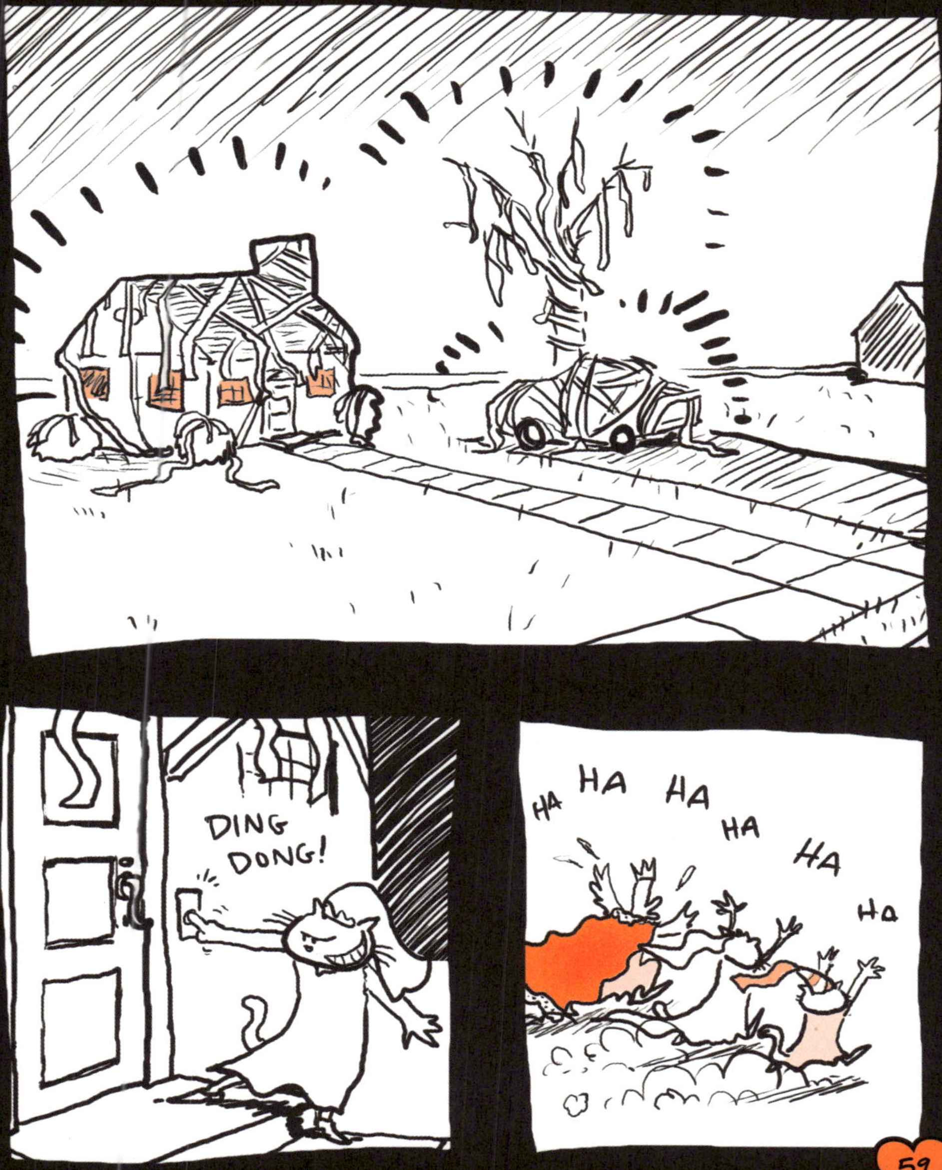
DING DONG!
HA HA HA HA HA HA

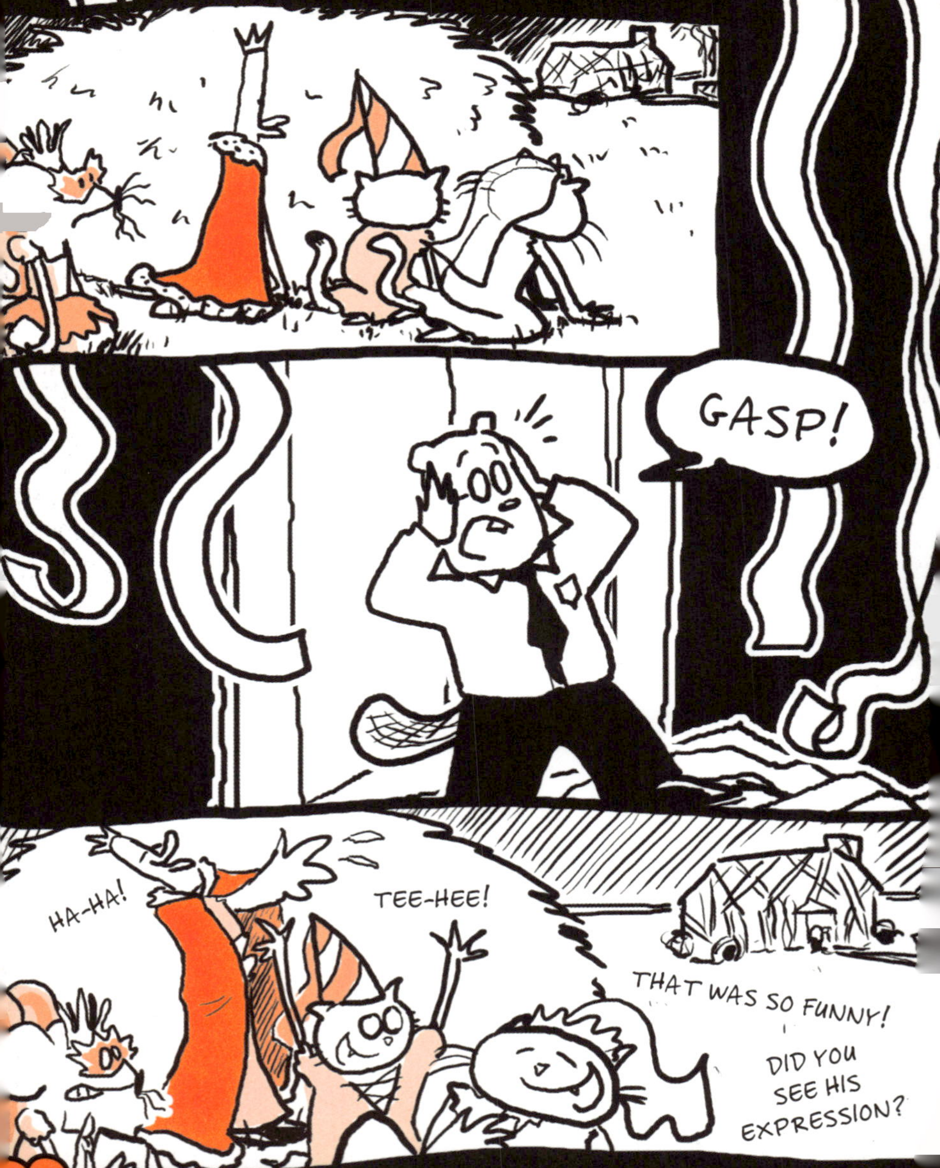
GASP!
HA-HA!
TEE-HEE!
THAT WAS SO FUNNY!
DID YOU SEE HIS EXPRESSION?

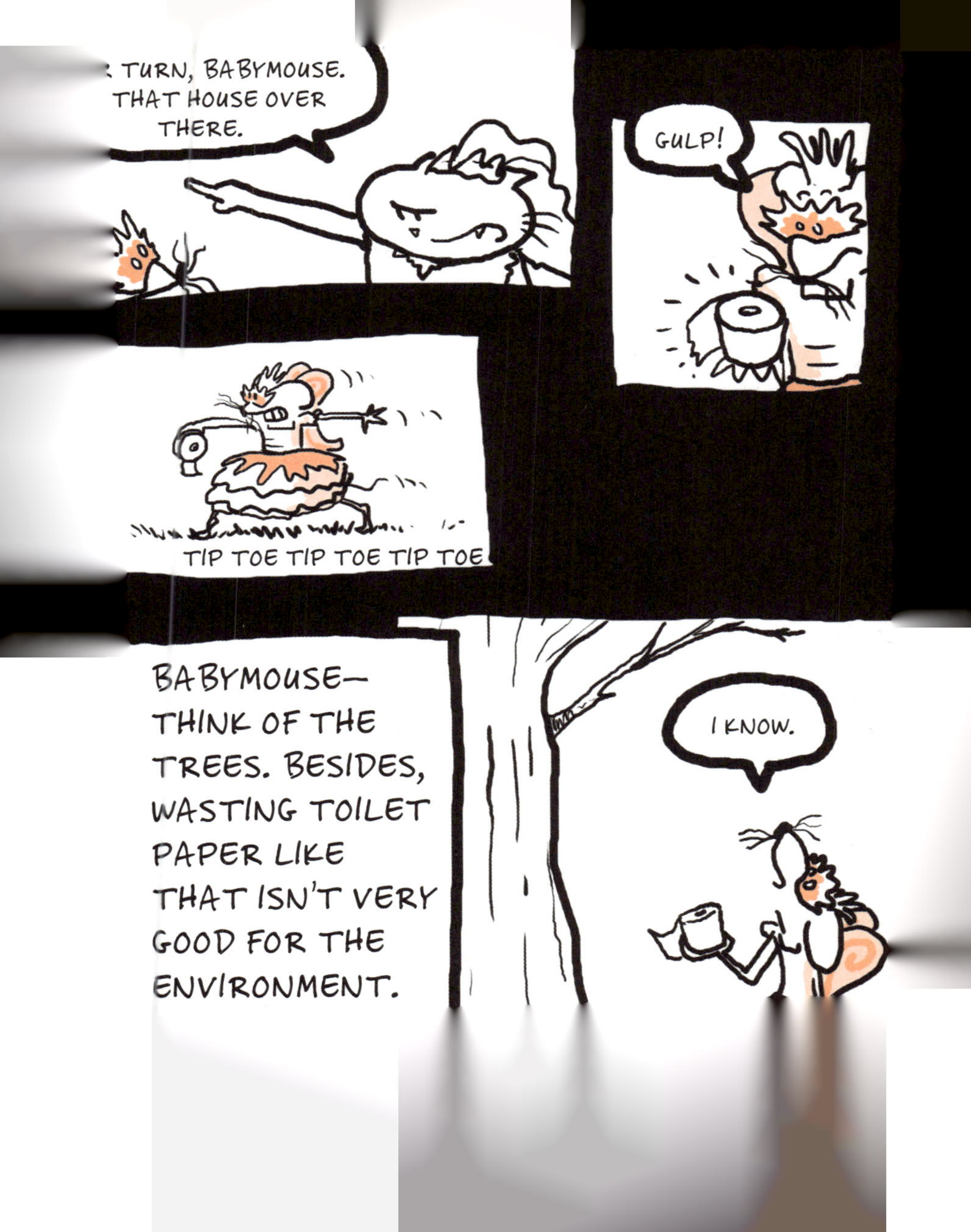

TURN, BABYMOUSE. THAT HOUSE OVER THERE.
GULP!
TIP TOE TIP TOE TIP TOE
BABYMOUSE— THINK OF THE TREES. BESIDES, WASTING TOILET PAPER LIKE THAT ISN'T VERY GOOD FOR THE ENVIRONMENT.
I KNOW.

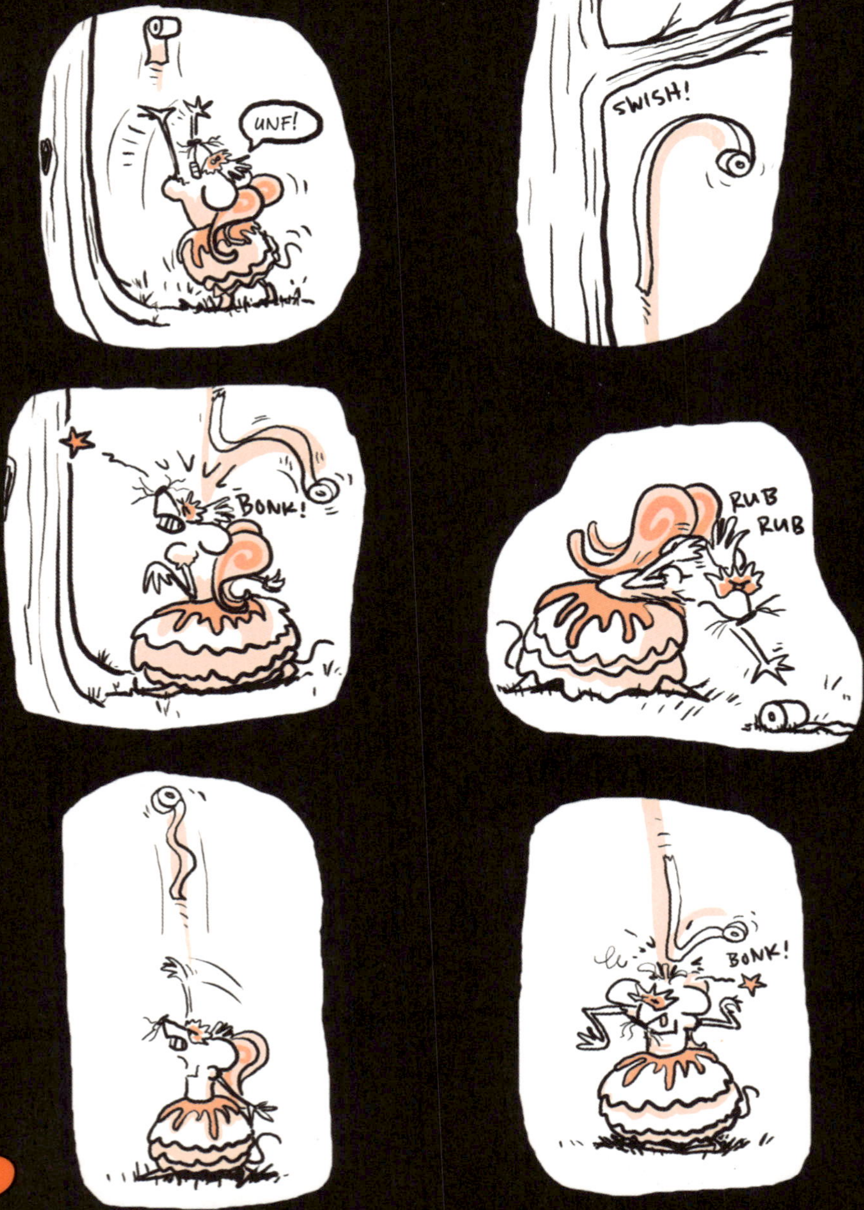
UNF!
SWISH!
BONK!
RUB
RUB
BONK!

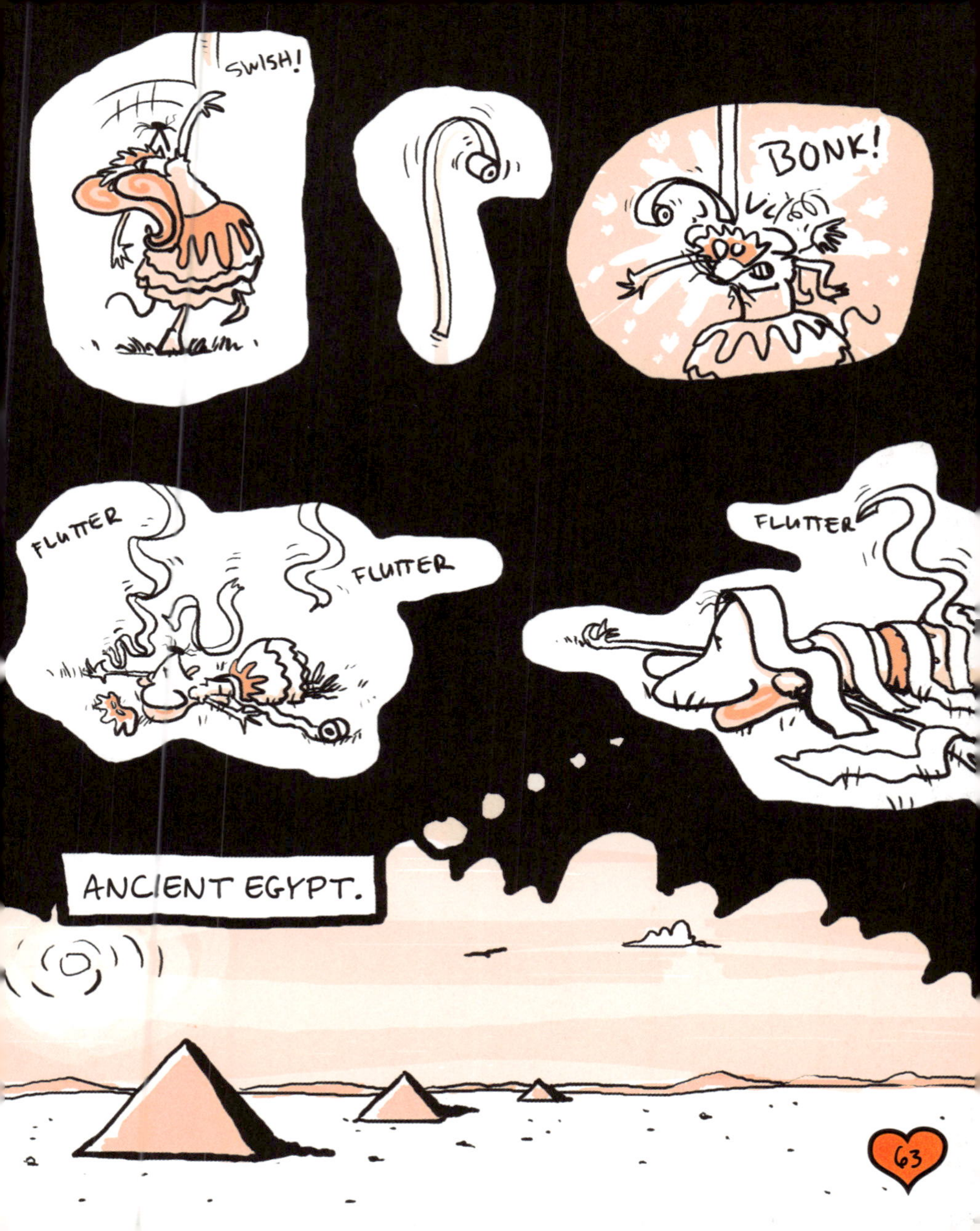
SWISH!
BONK!
FLUTTER
FLUTTER
FLUTTER
ANCIENT EGYPT.

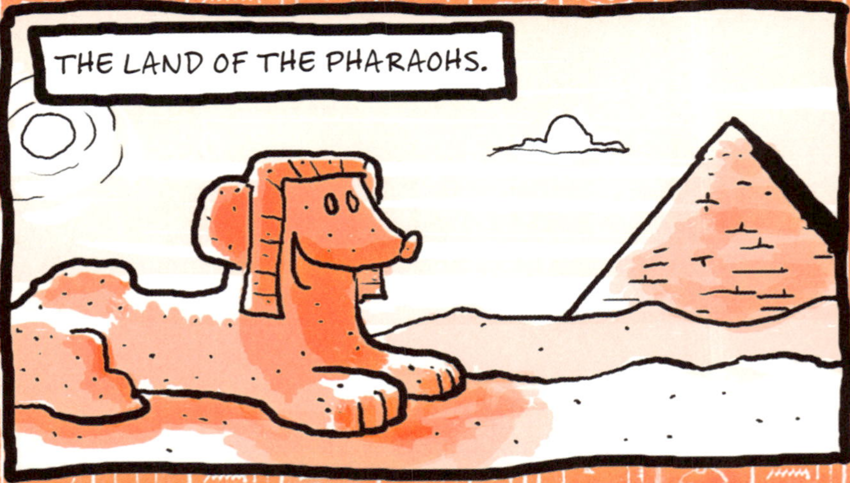
THE LAND OF THE PHARAOHS.

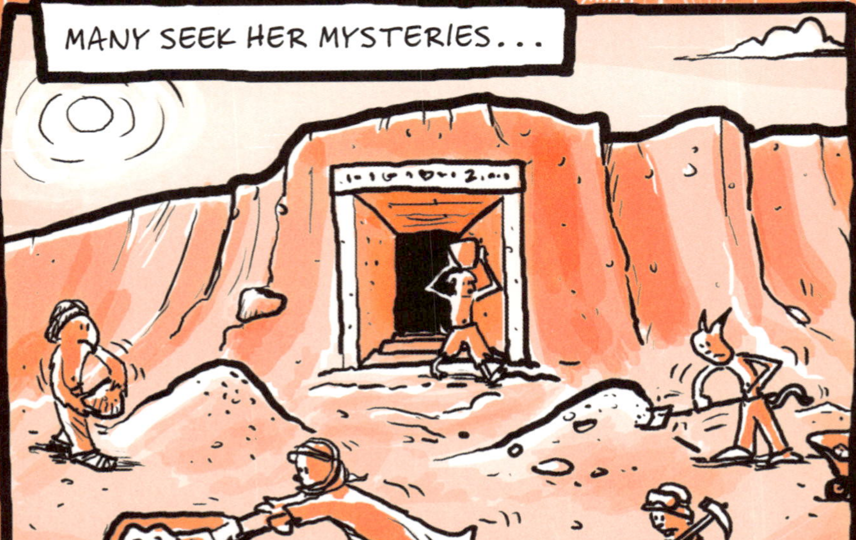
MANY SEEK HER MYSTERIES...

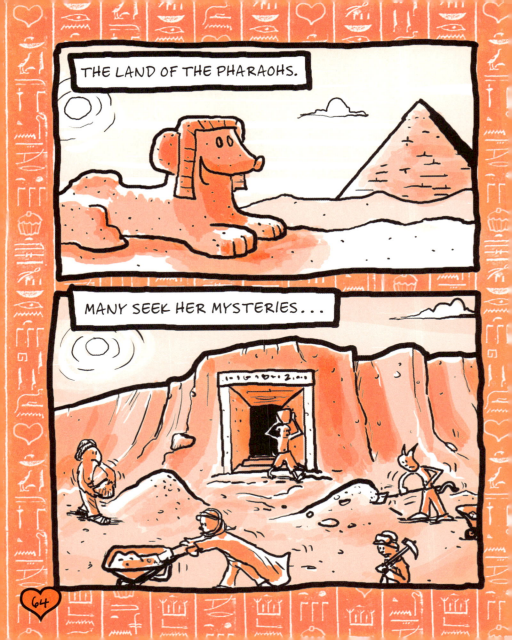

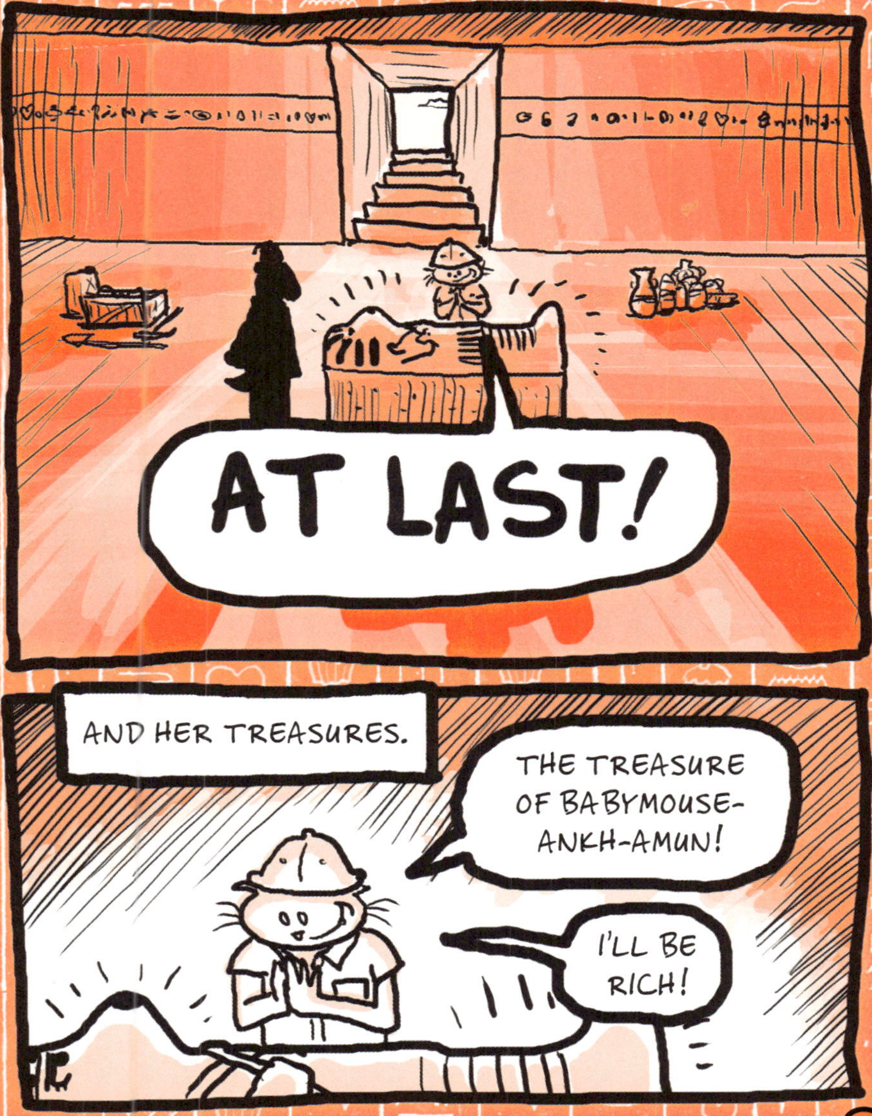
AT LAST!
AND HER TREASURES.
THE TREASURE OF BABYMOUSE-ANKH-AMUN!
I'LL BE RICH!

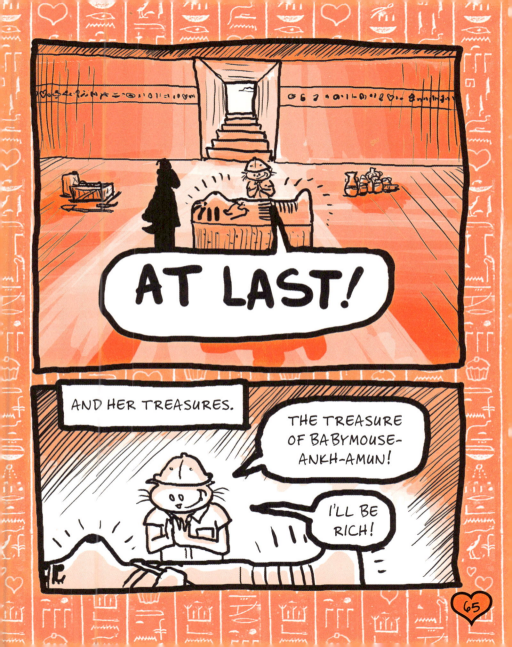

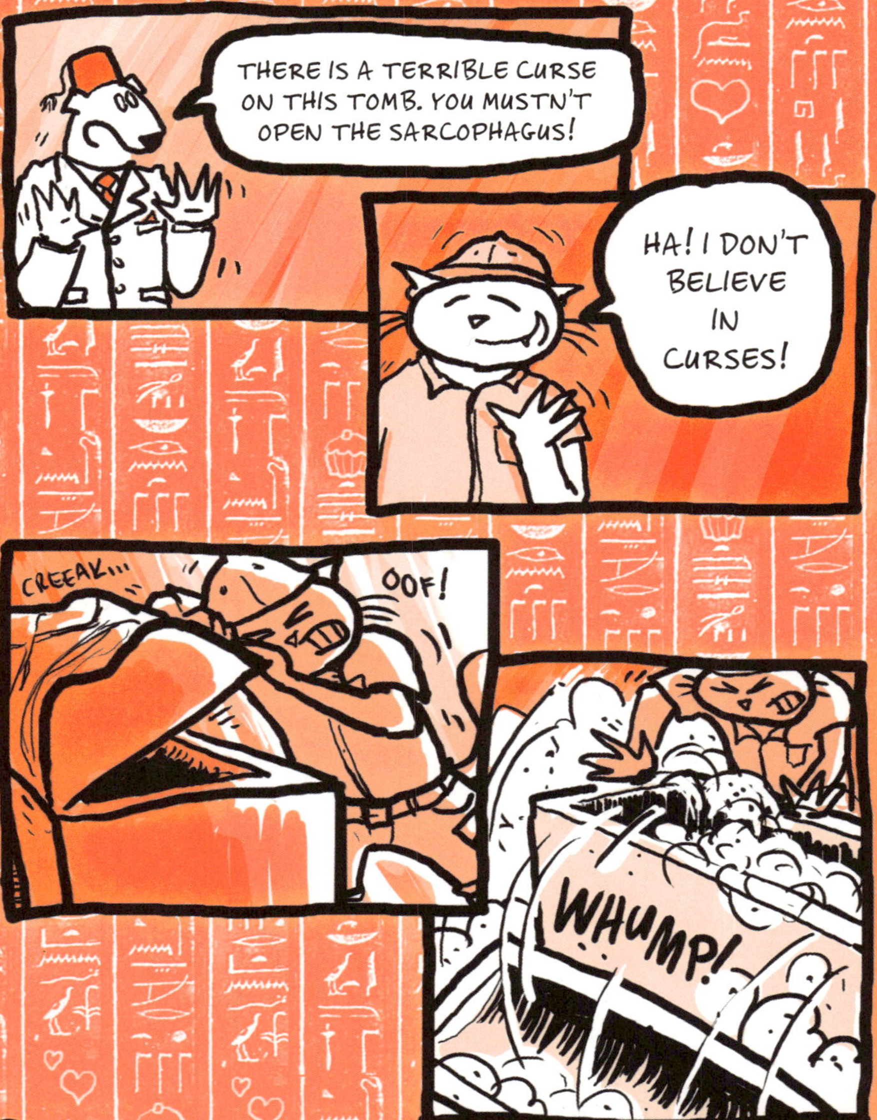
THERE IS A TERRIBLE CURSE ON THIS TOMB. YOU MUSTN'T OPEN THE SARCOPHAGUS!
HA! I DON'T BELIEVE IN CURSES!
CREEAK...
OOF!
WHUMP!

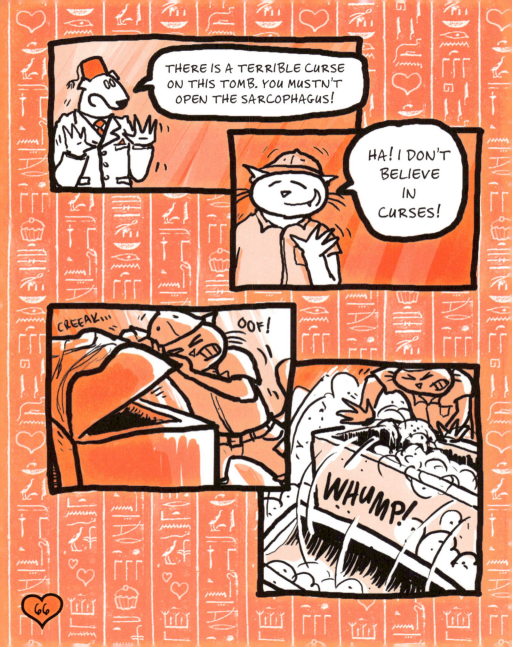

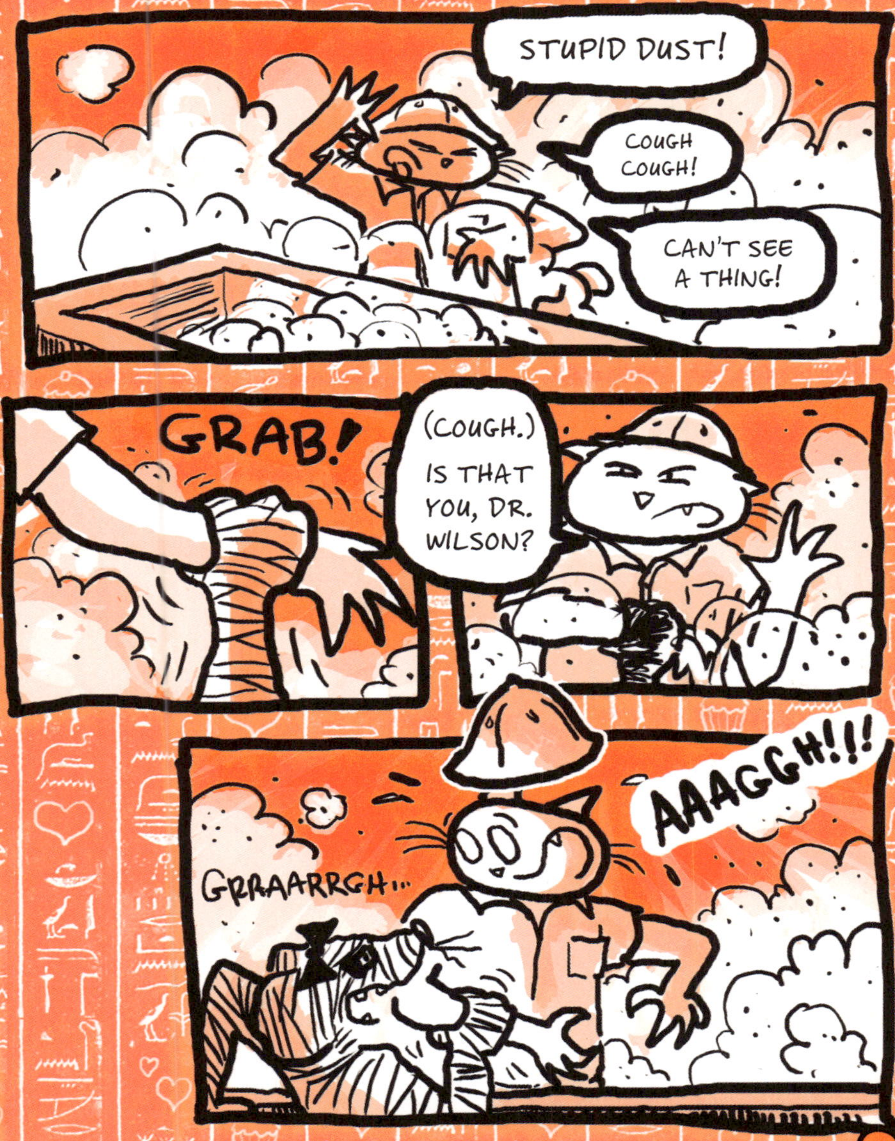
STUPID DUST!
COUGH COUGH!
CAN'T SEE A THING!
GRAB!
(COUGH.) IS THAT YOU, DR. WILSON?
GRRAARRGH...
AAAGGH!!!

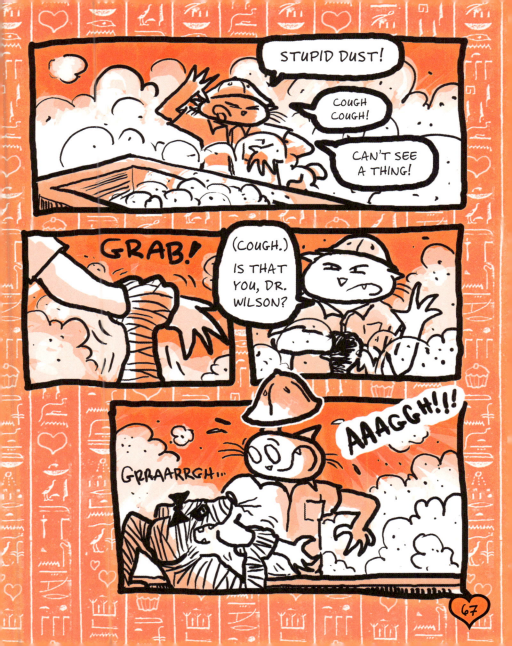

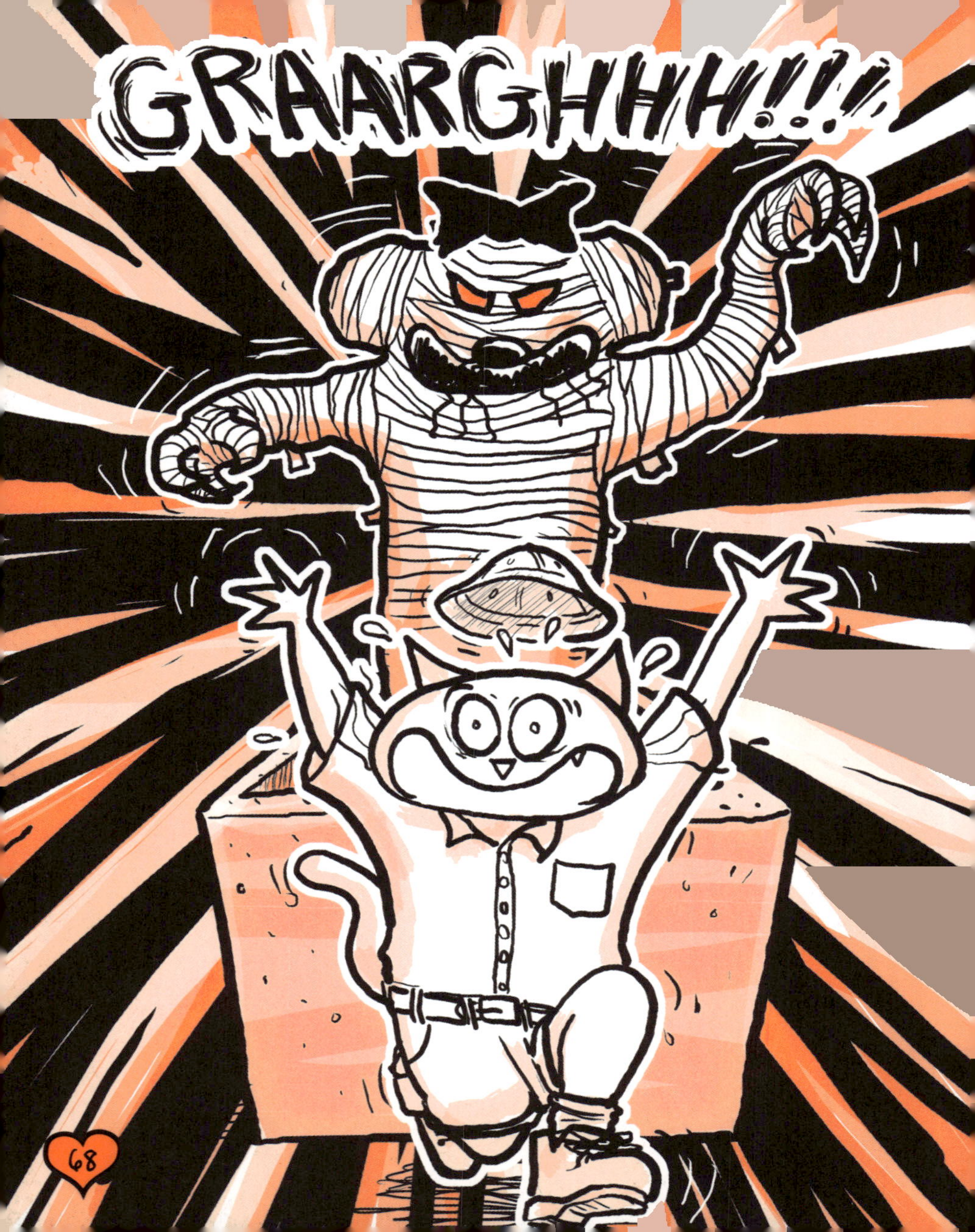
GRAARGHHHH!!!

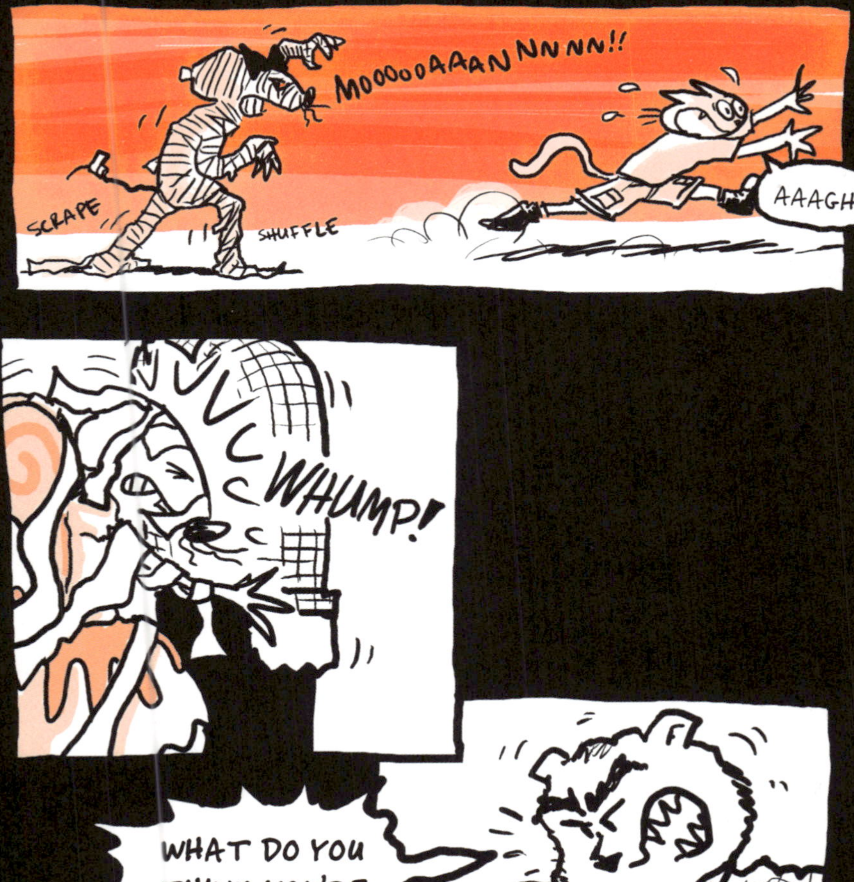
MOOOOOAAANNNNN!!
SCRAPE
SHUFFLE
AAAGH!
WHUMP!
WHAT DO YOU THINK YOU'RE DOING TO MY YARD?!?!
!

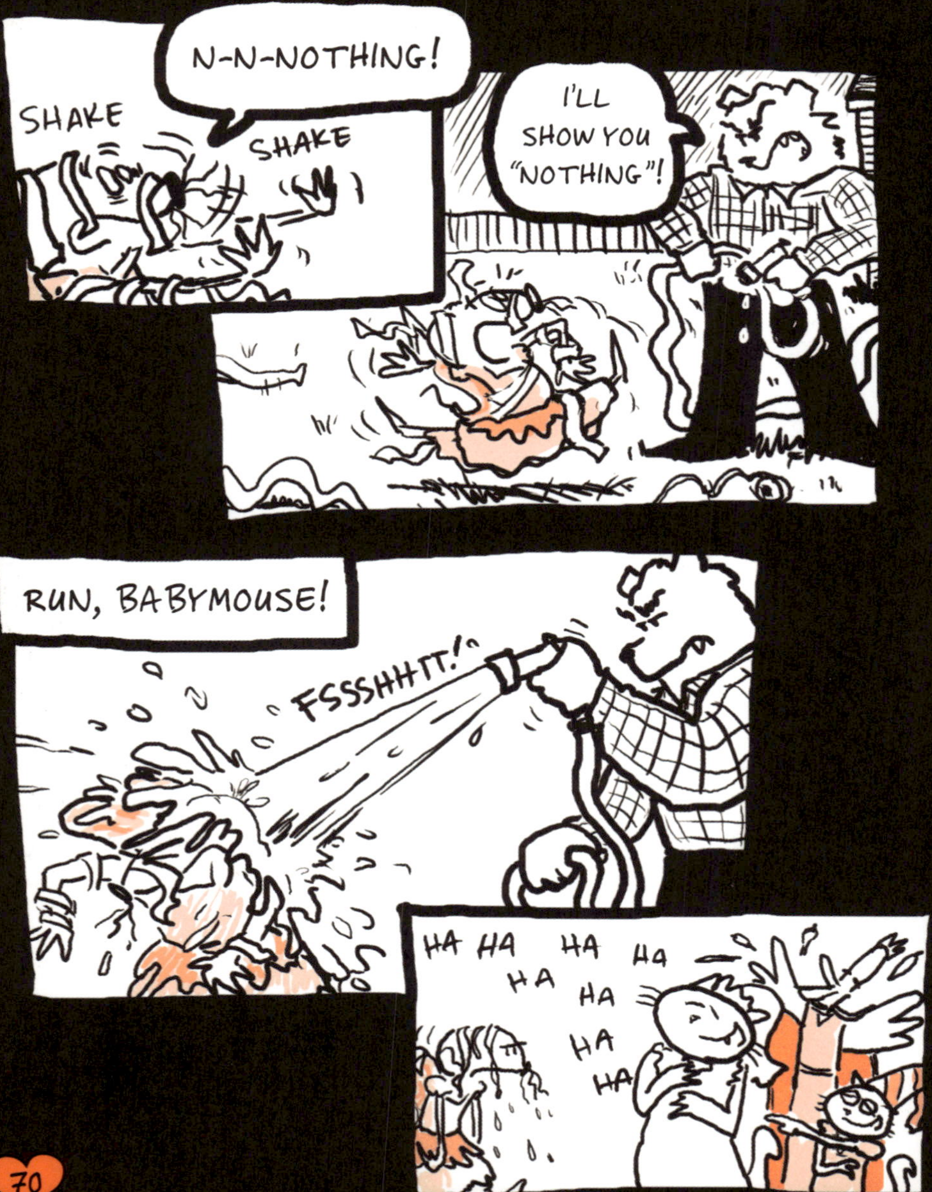
N-N-NOTHING!
SHAKE
SHAKE
I'LL SHOW YOU "NOTHING"!
RUN, BABYMOUSE!
FSSSHHTT!
HA HA HA HA HA HA HA HA

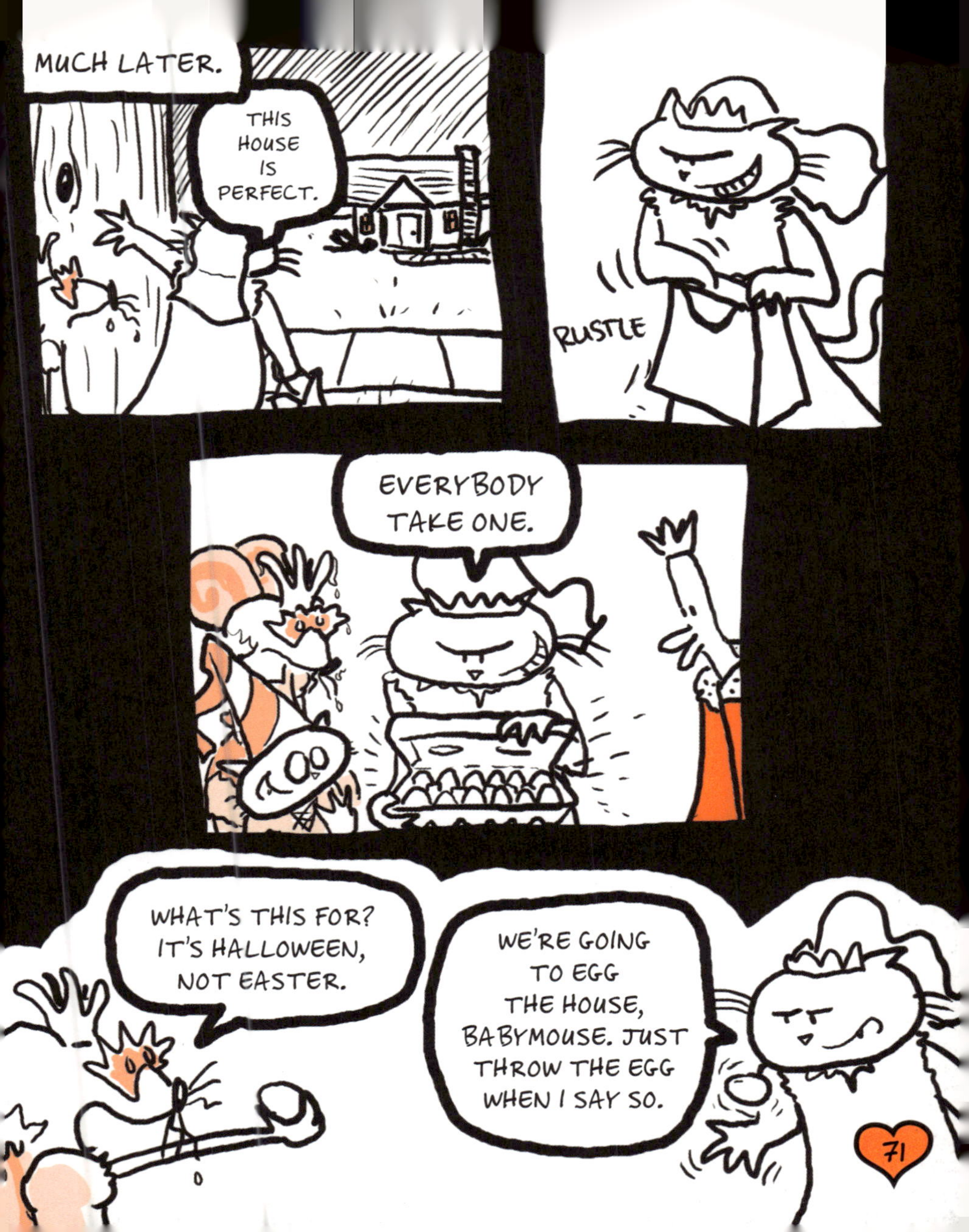

MUCH LATER.
THIS HOUSE IS PERFECT.
RUSTLE
EVERYBODY TAKE ONE.
WHAT'S THIS FOR? IT'S HALLOWEEN, NOT EASTER.
WE'RE GOING TO EGG THE HOUSE, BABYMOUSE. JUST THROW THE EGG WHEN I SAY SO.

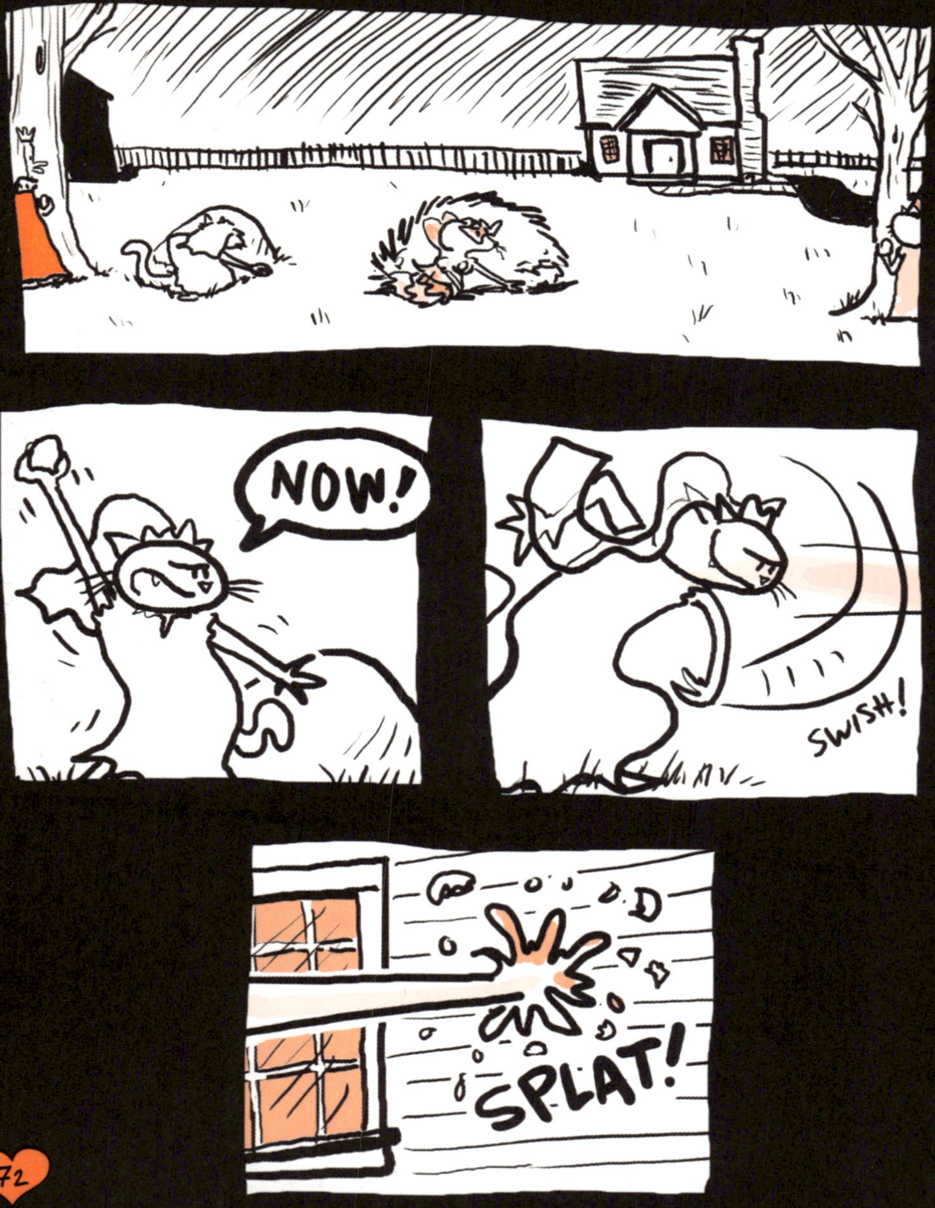
NOW!
SWISH!
SPLAT!

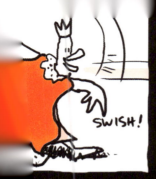

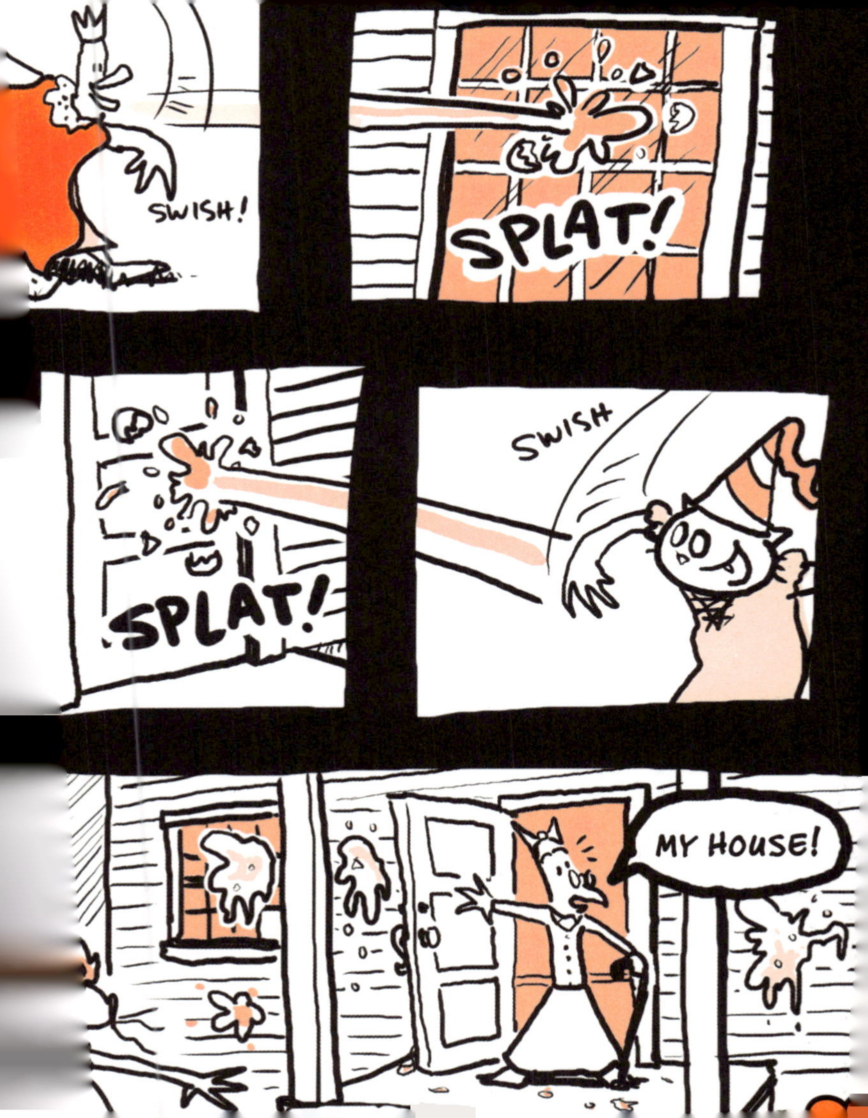
SWISH!
SPLAT!
SPLAT!
SWISH
MY HOUSE!

PSST! HURRY! THROW THE EGG, BABYMOUSE!

FLING!

SPLAT!

I USED T[O] REALL[Y] LIKE HALLOWE[EN] BEFOR[E] TONIGH[T]

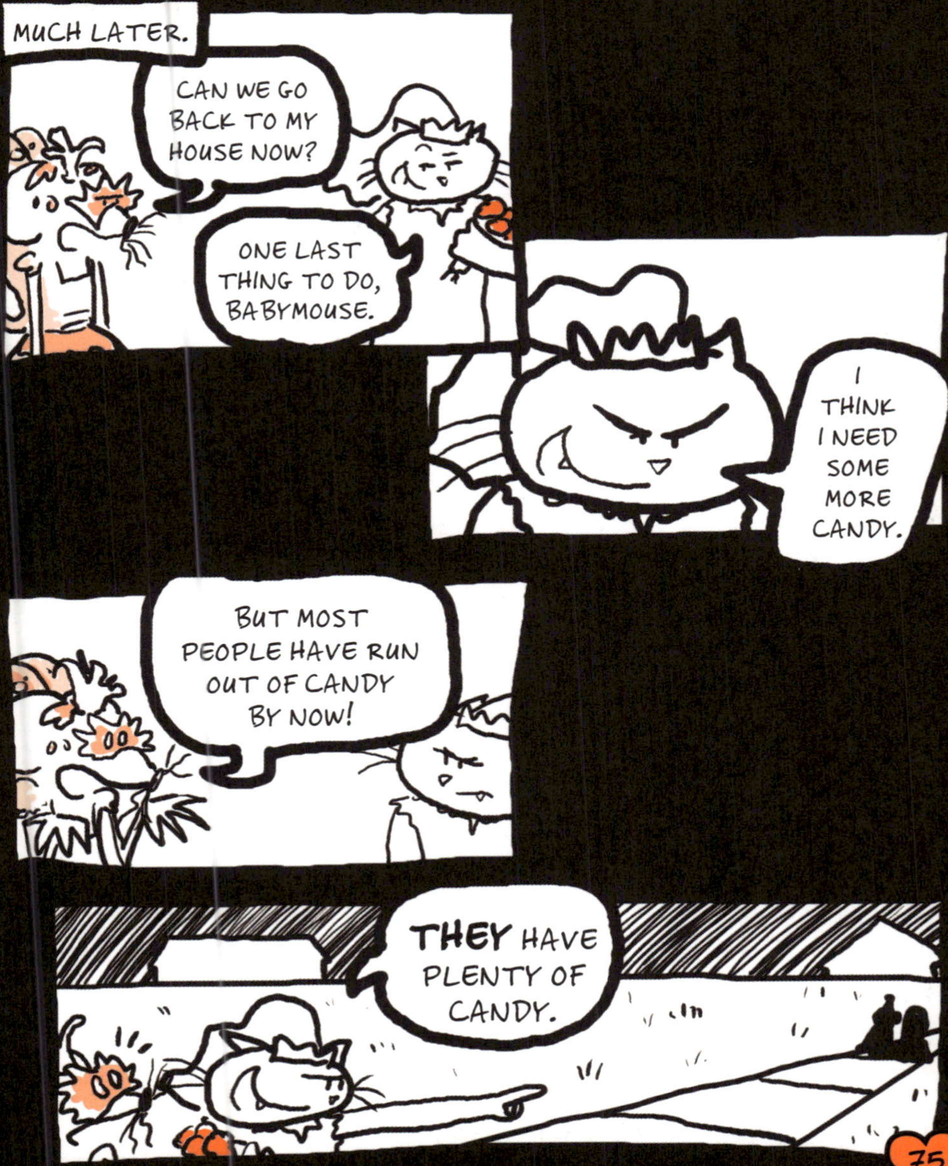
MUCH LATER.
CAN WE GO BACK TO MY HOUSE NOW?
ONE LAST THING TO DO, BABYMOUSE.
I THINK I NEED SOME MORE CANDY.
BUT MOST PEOPLE HAVE RUN OUT OF CANDY BY NOW!
THEY HAVE PLENTY OF CANDY.

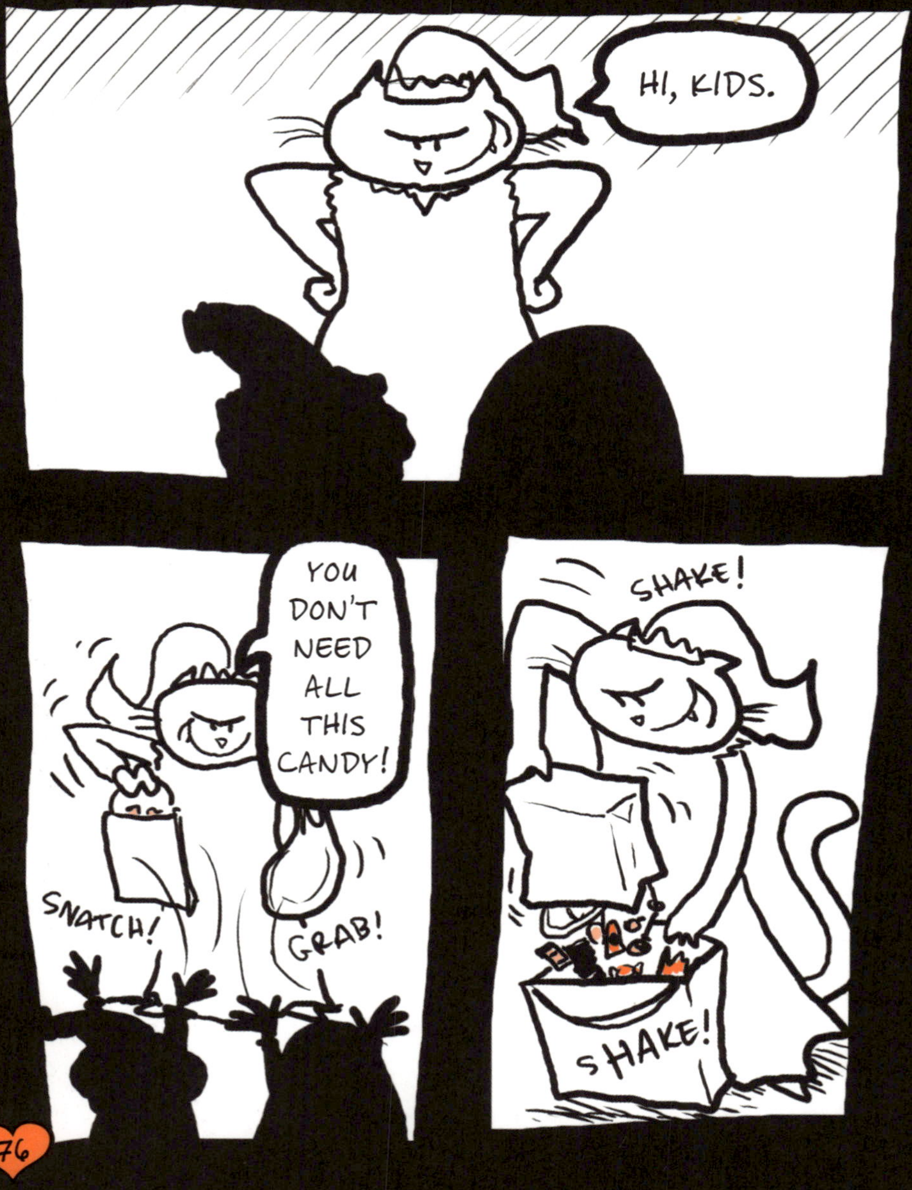
HI, KIDS.
YOU DON'T NEED ALL THIS CANDY!
SNATCH!
GRAB!
SHAKE!
SHAKE!

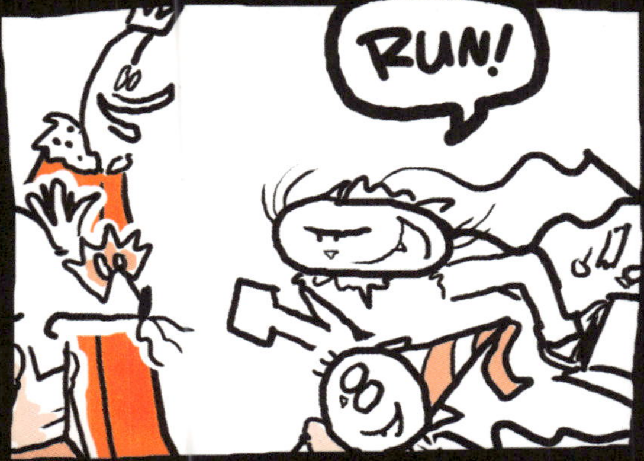
RUN!

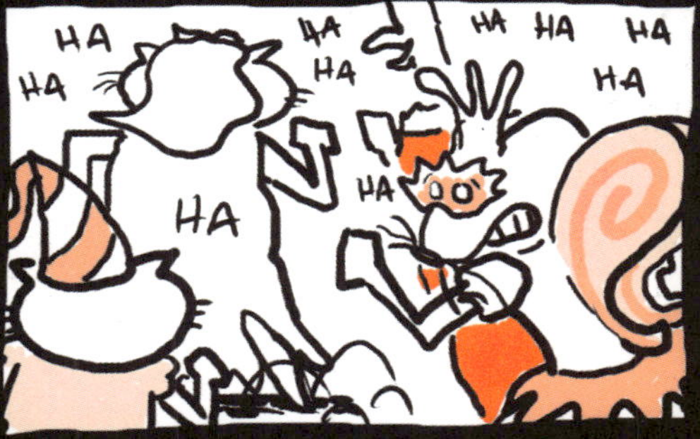
HA
HA
HA
HA
HA HA HA
HA
HA
HA

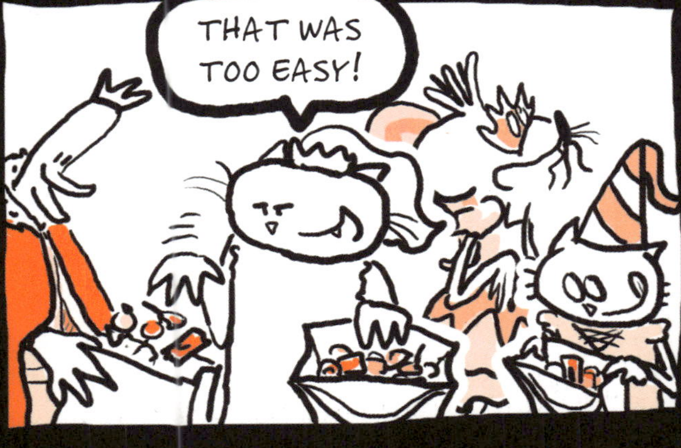
THAT WAS TOO EASY!

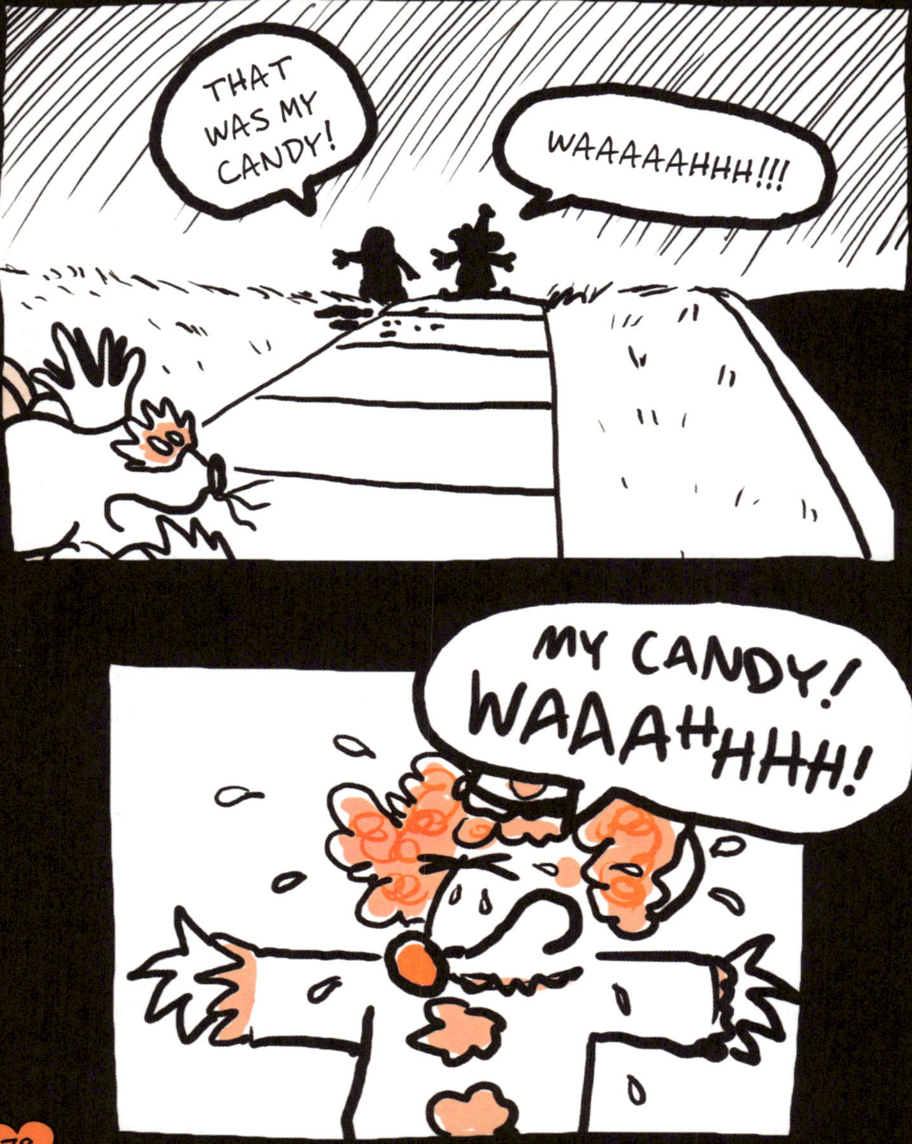
THAT WAS MY CANDY!
WAAAAAAHHH!!!
MY CANDY! WAAAHHHH!

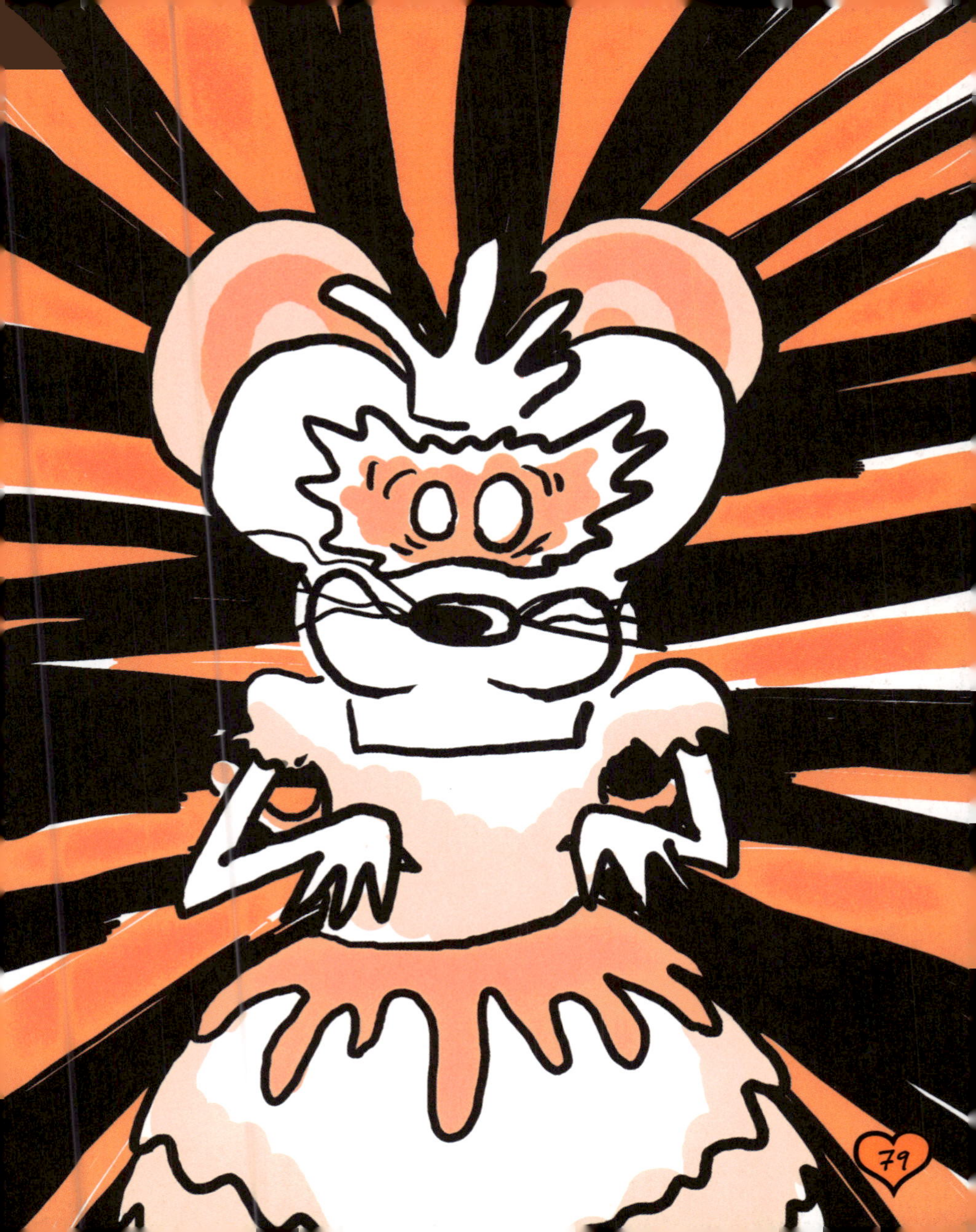

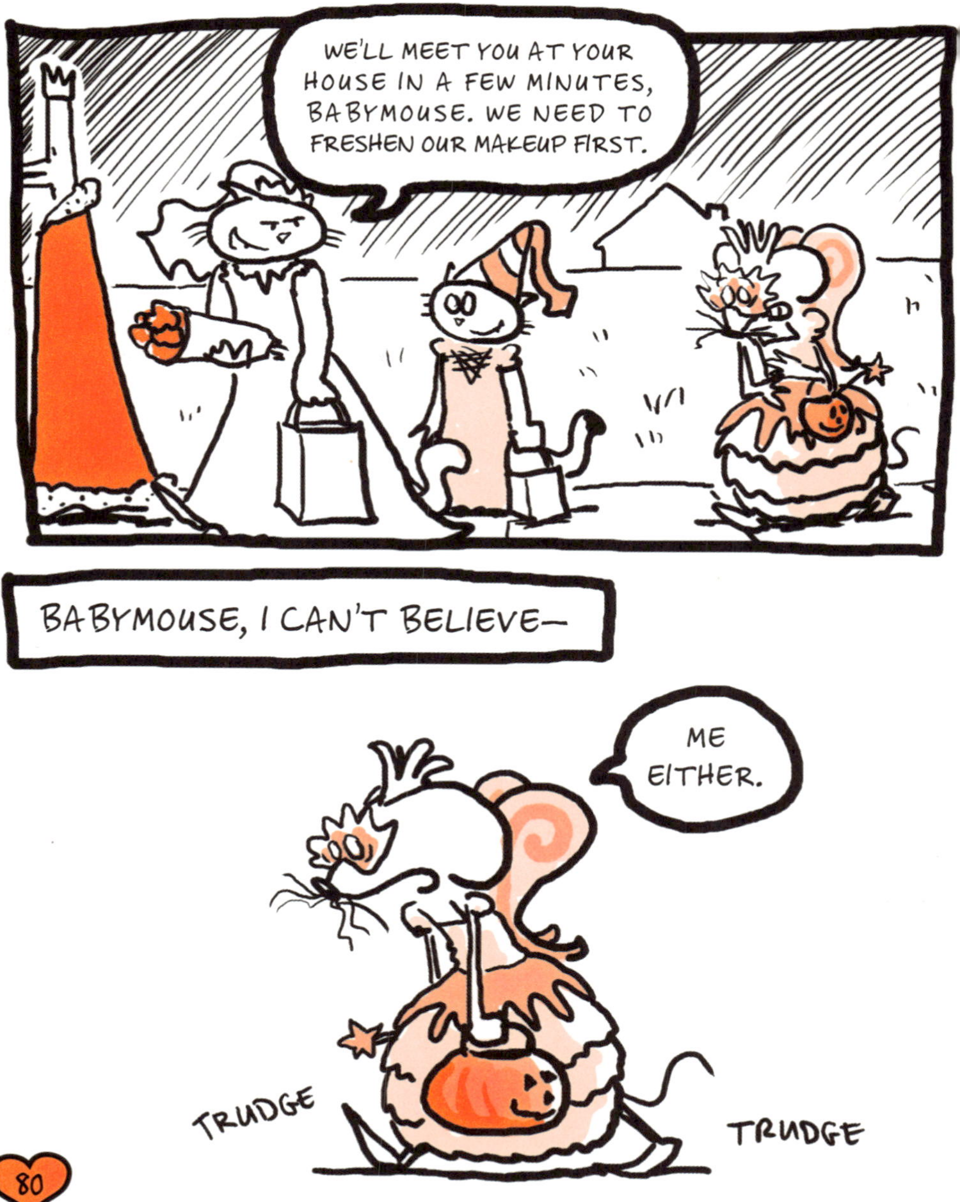
WE'LL MEET YOU AT YOUR HOUSE IN A FEW MINUTES, BABYMOUSE. WE NEED TO FRESHEN OUR MAKEUP FIRST.
BABYMOUSE, I CAN'T BELIEVE—
ME EITHER.
TRUDGE
TRUDGE

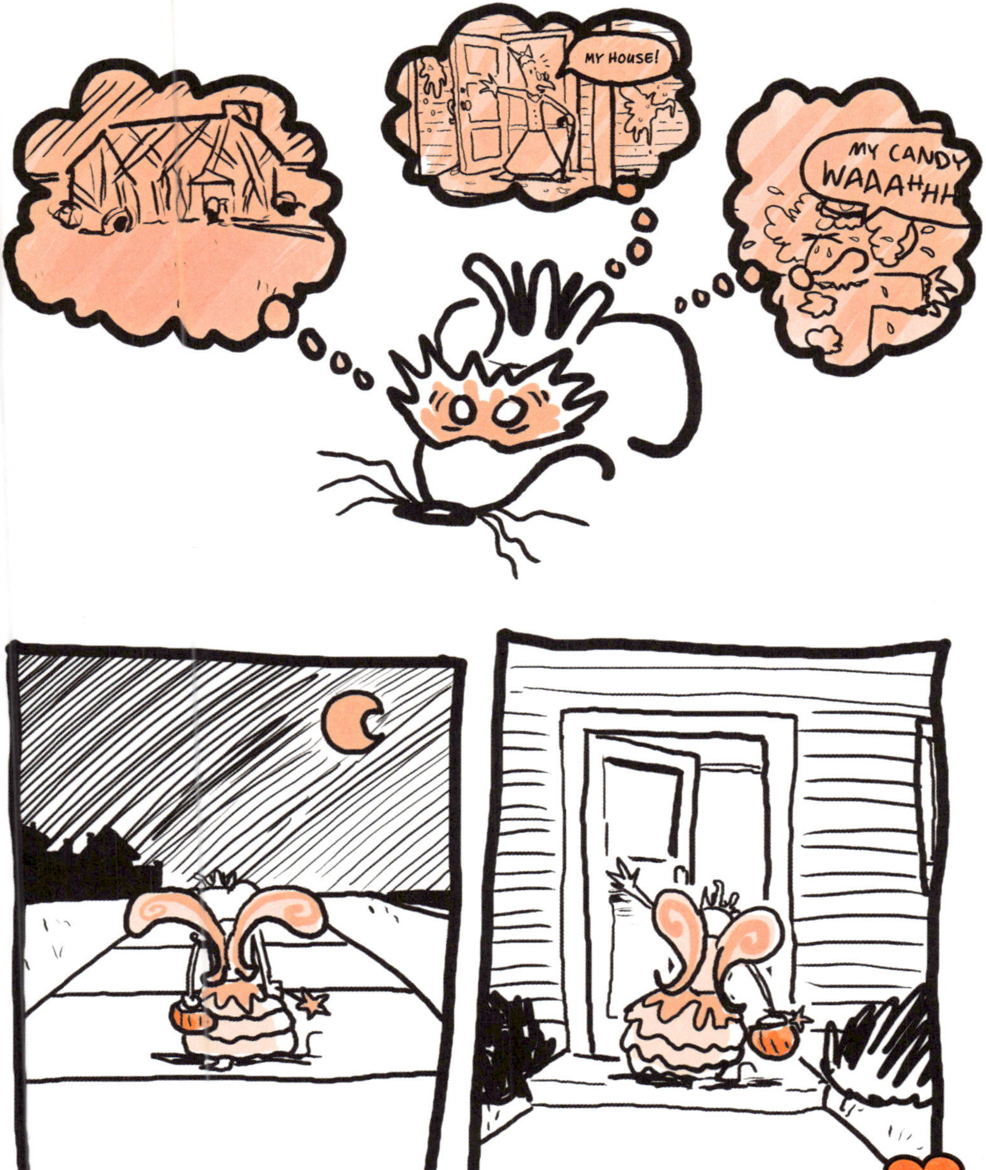
MY HOUSE!
MY CANDY
WAAAHHH

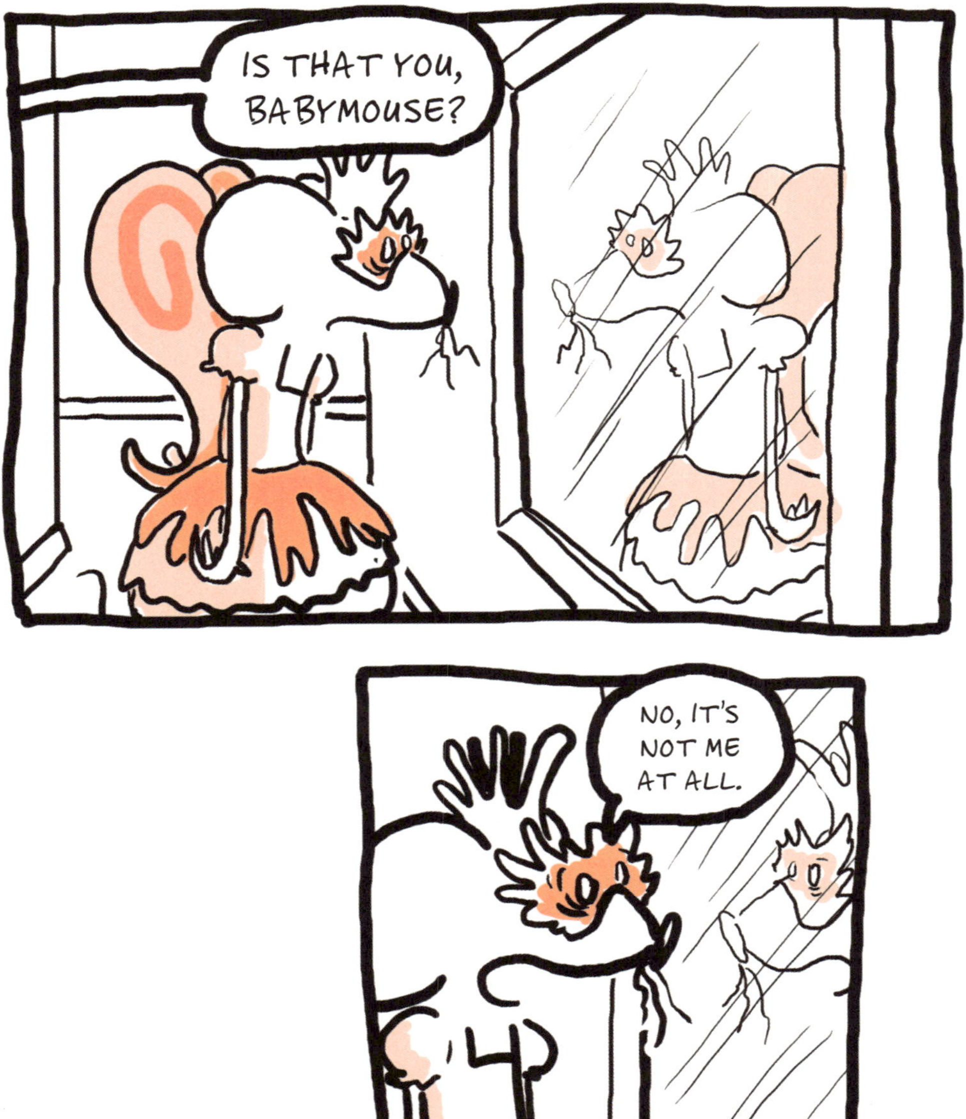
IS THAT YOU, BABYMOUSE?
NO, IT'S NOT ME AT ALL.

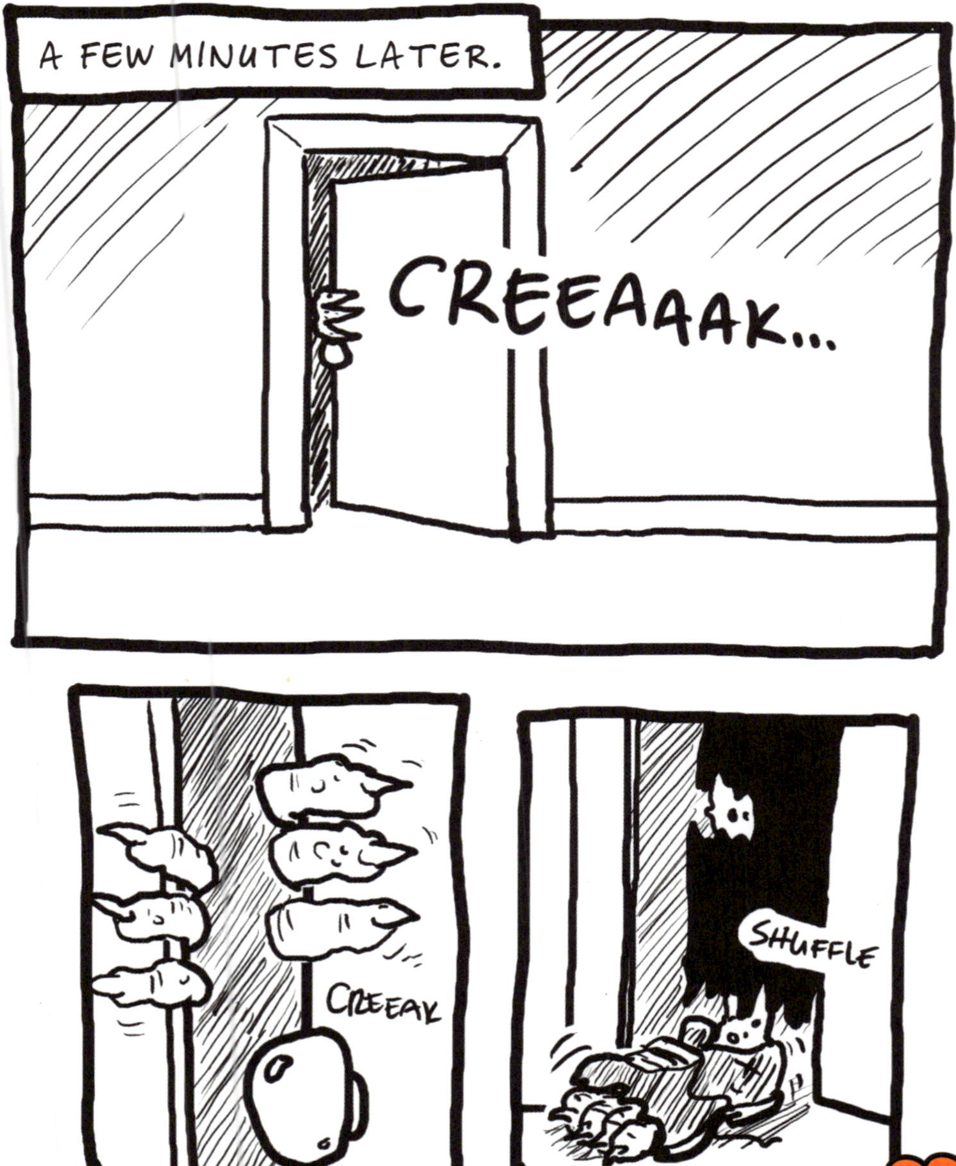
A FEW MINUTES LATER.
CREEAAAK...
CREEAK
SHUFFLE

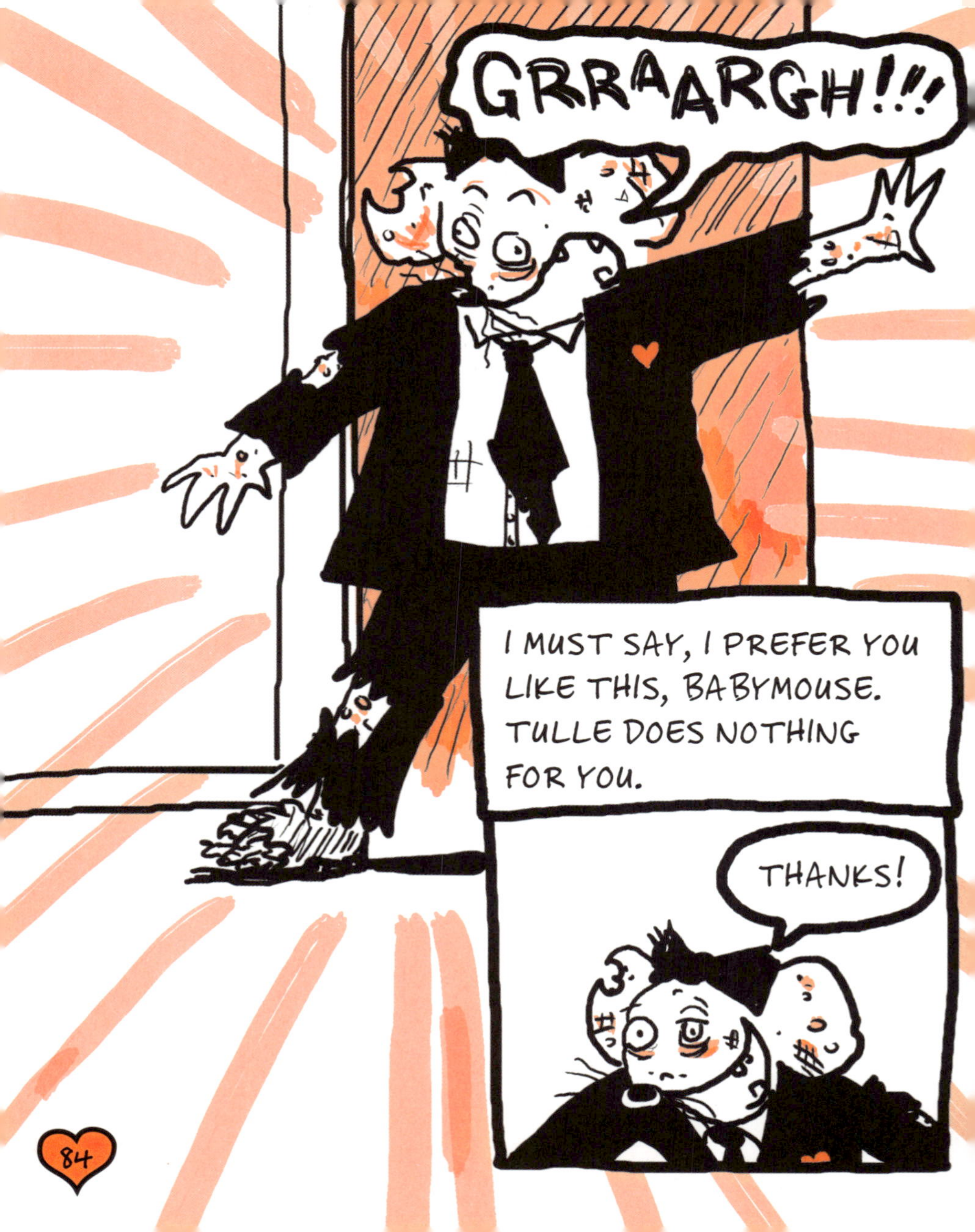
GRRAARGH!!!
I MUST SAY, I PREFER YOU LIKE THIS, BABYMOUSE. TULLE DOES NOTHING FOR YOU.
THANKS!

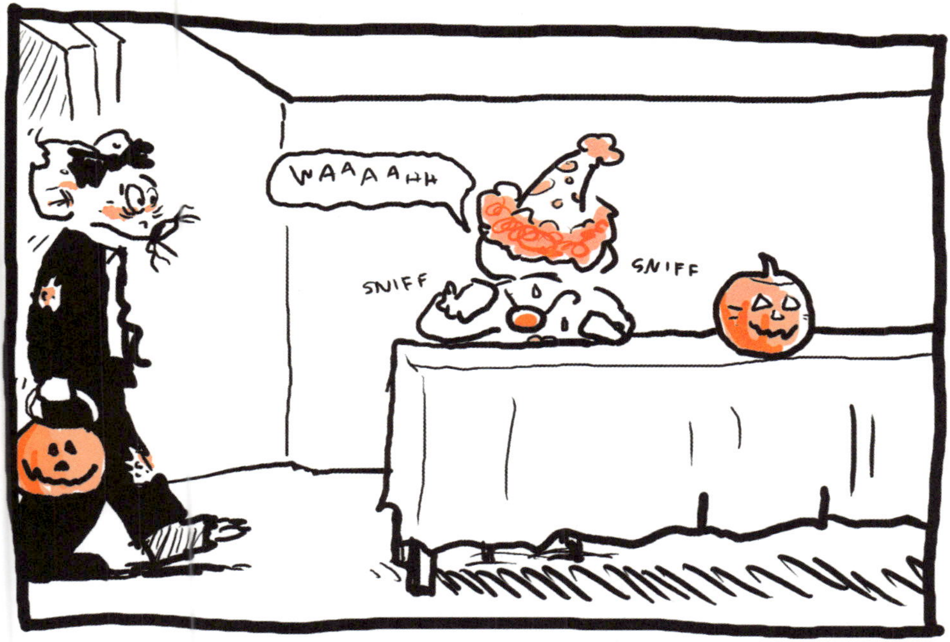
WAAAAHH
SNIFF
SNIFF

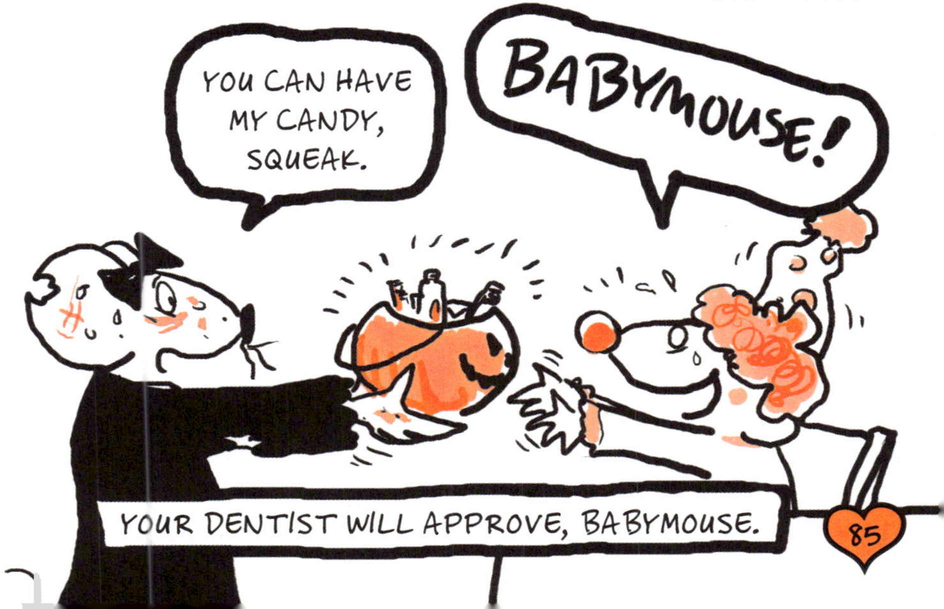
YOU CAN HAVE MY CANDY, SQUEAK.
BABYMOUSE!
YOUR DENTIST WILL APPROVE, BABYMOUSE.
85

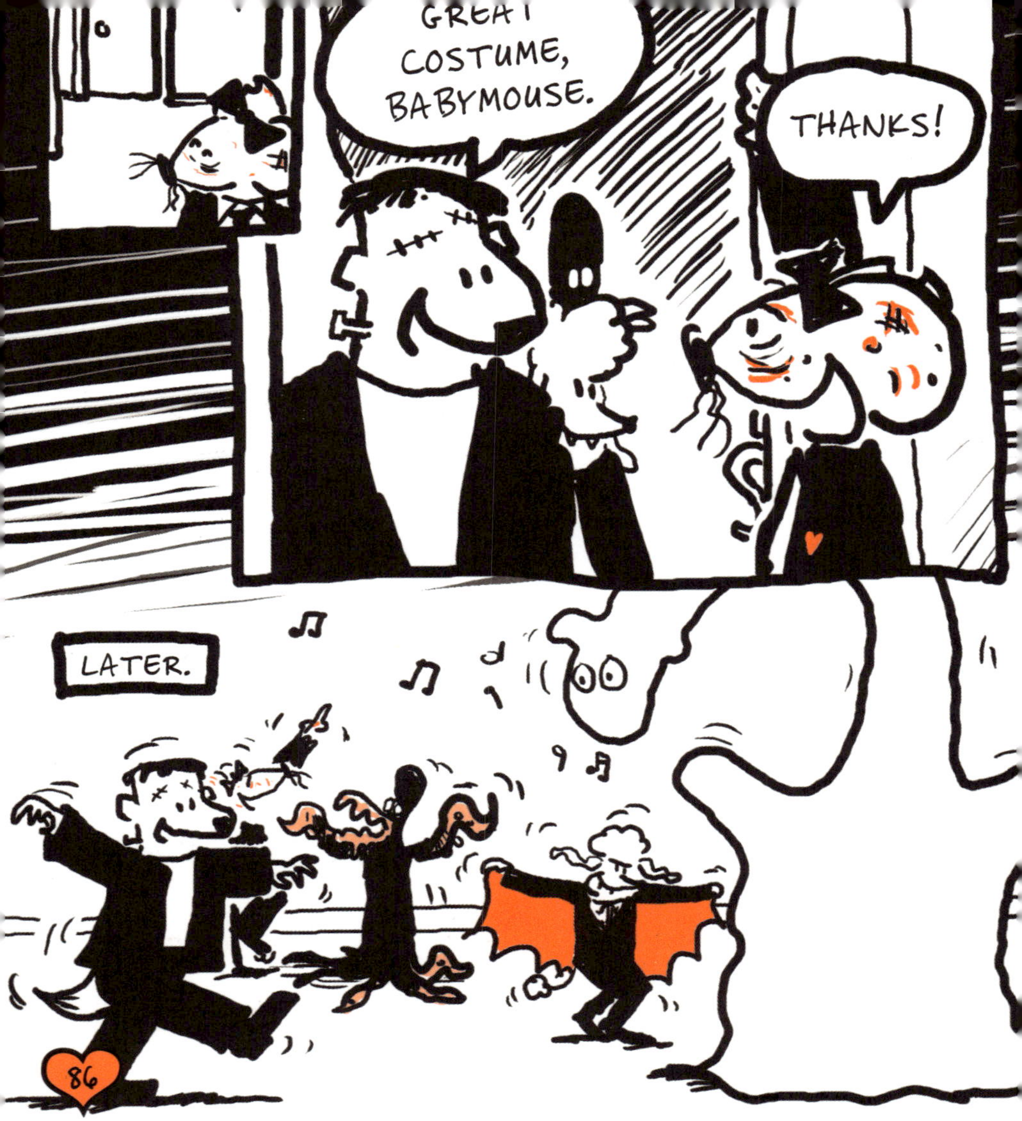
COSTUME, BABYMOUSE.
THANKS!
LATER.

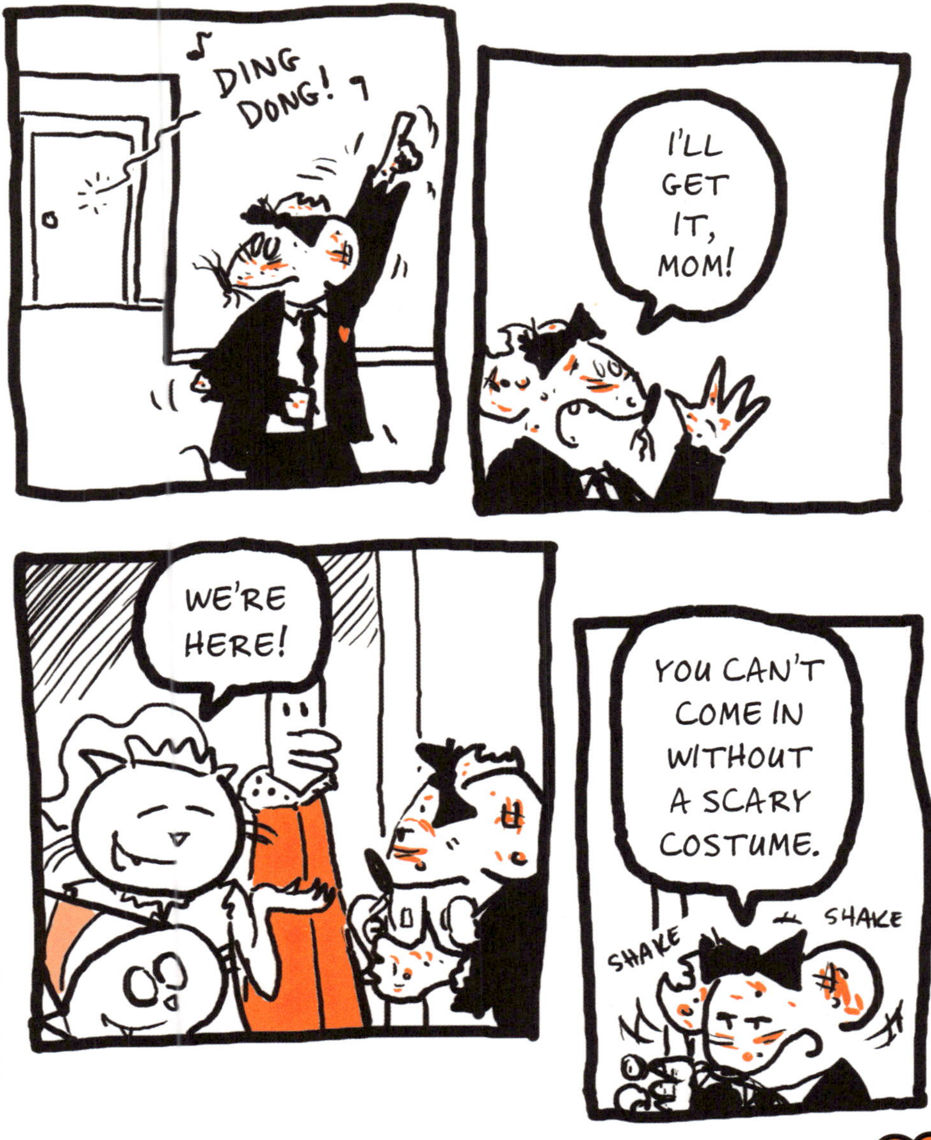
DING DONG!
I'LL GET IT, MOM!
WE'RE HERE!
YOU CAN'T COME IN WITHOUT A SCARY COSTUME.
SHAKE
SHAKE

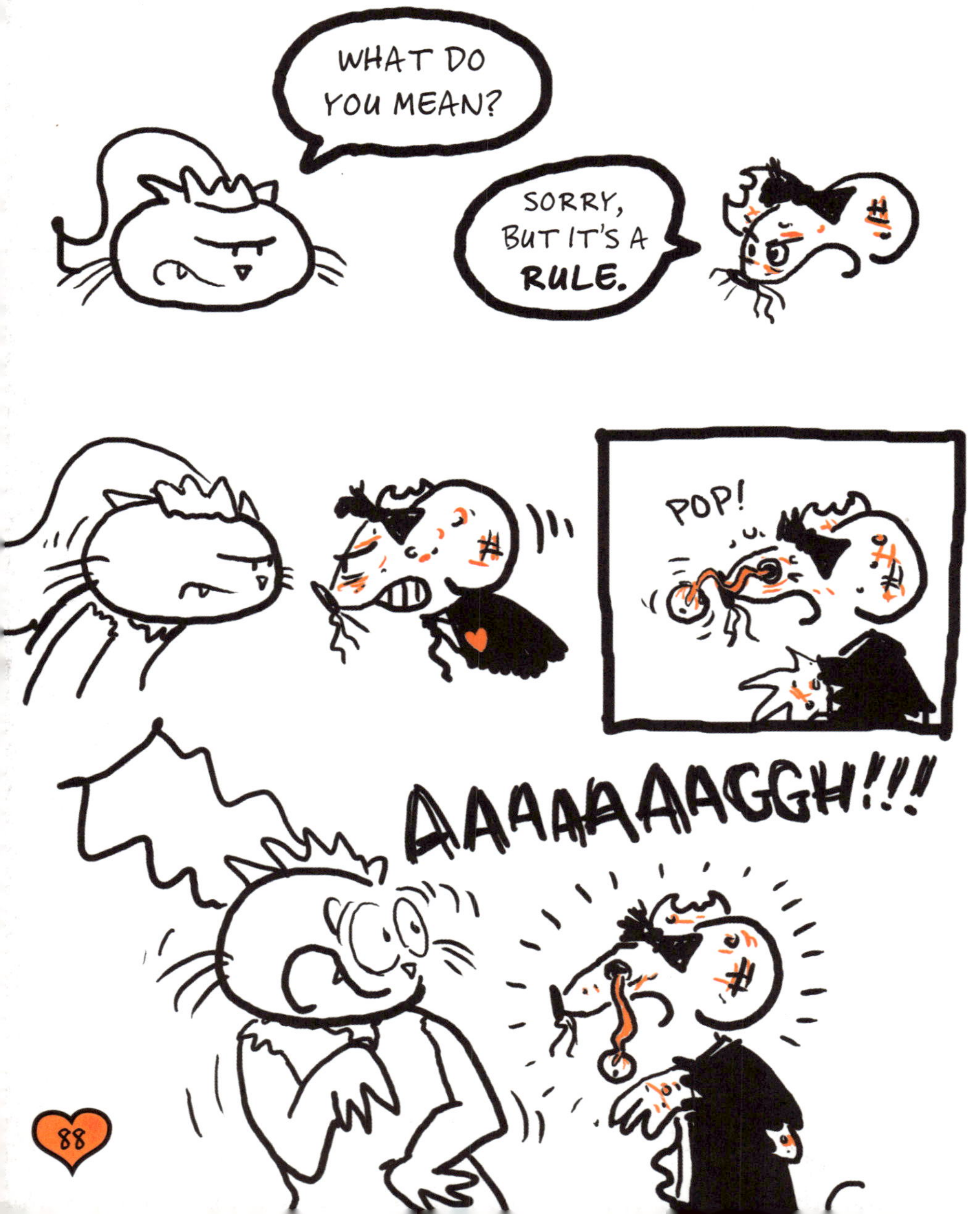
WHAT DO YOU MEAN?
SORRY, BUT IT'S A **RULE.**
POP!
AAAAAAAGGH!!!!

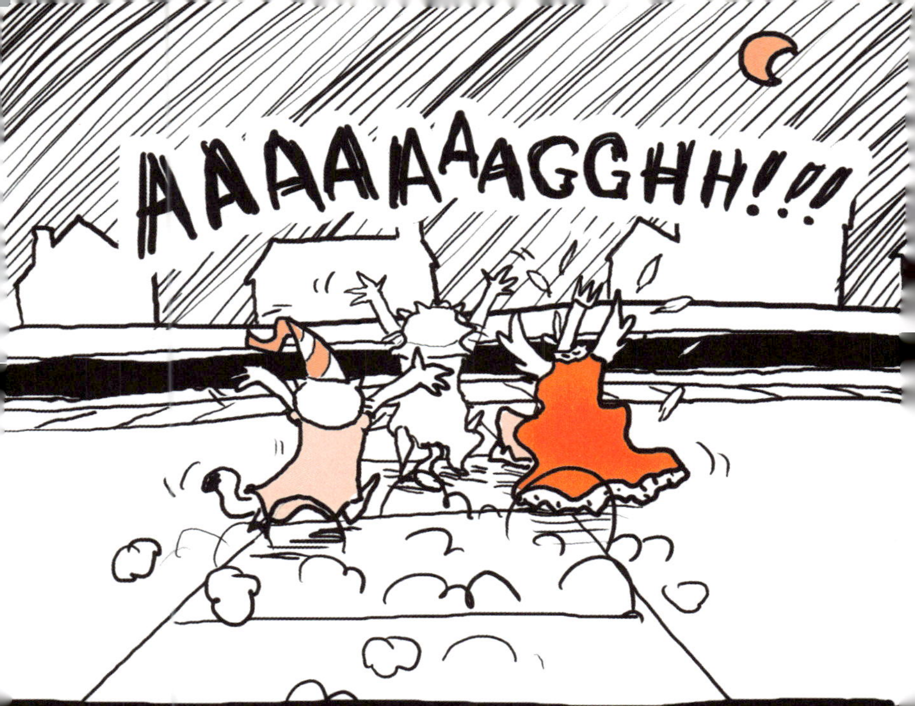
AAAAAAAGGHH!!!!

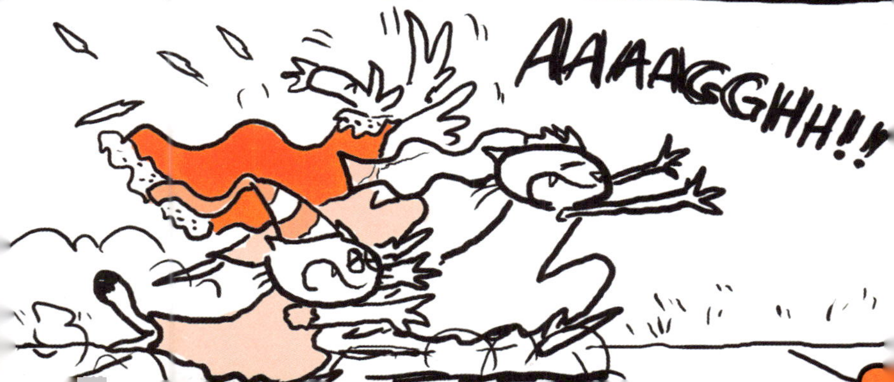
AAAAGGHH!!!

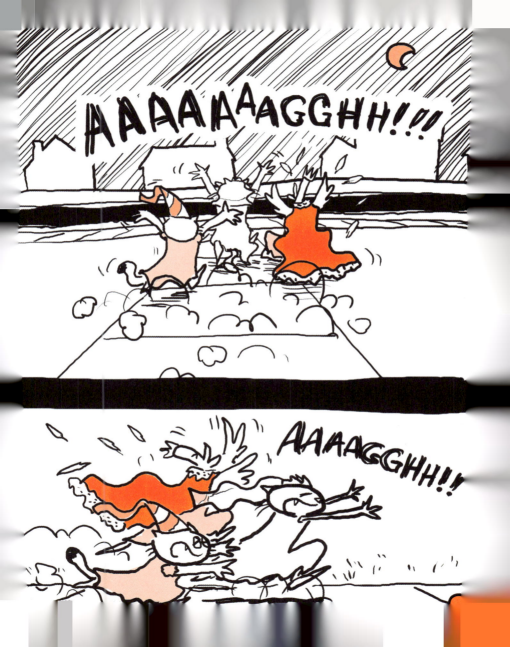

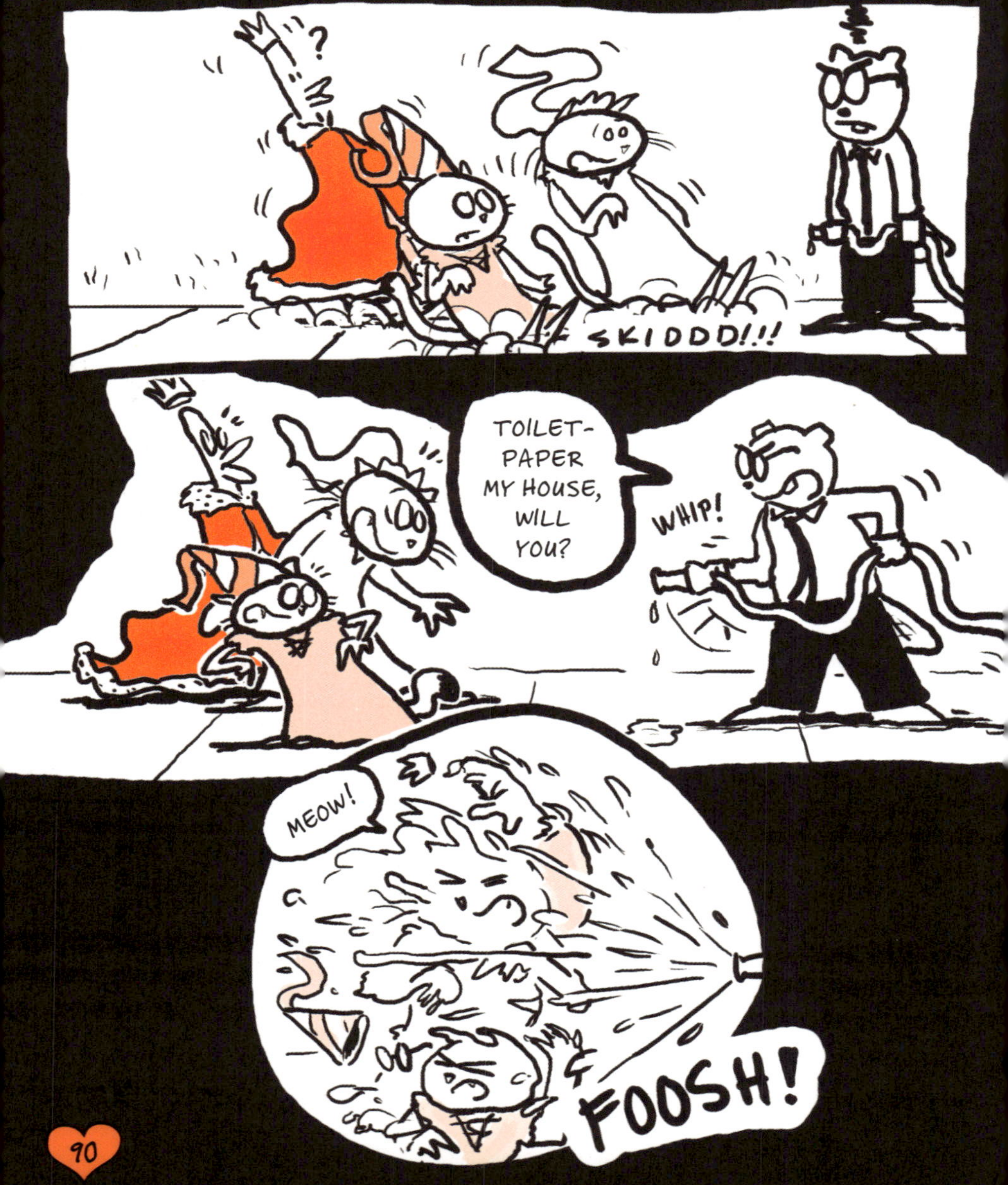
?
SKIDDD!!!
TOILET-PAPER MY HOUSE, WILL YOU?
WHIP!
MEOW!
FOOSH!

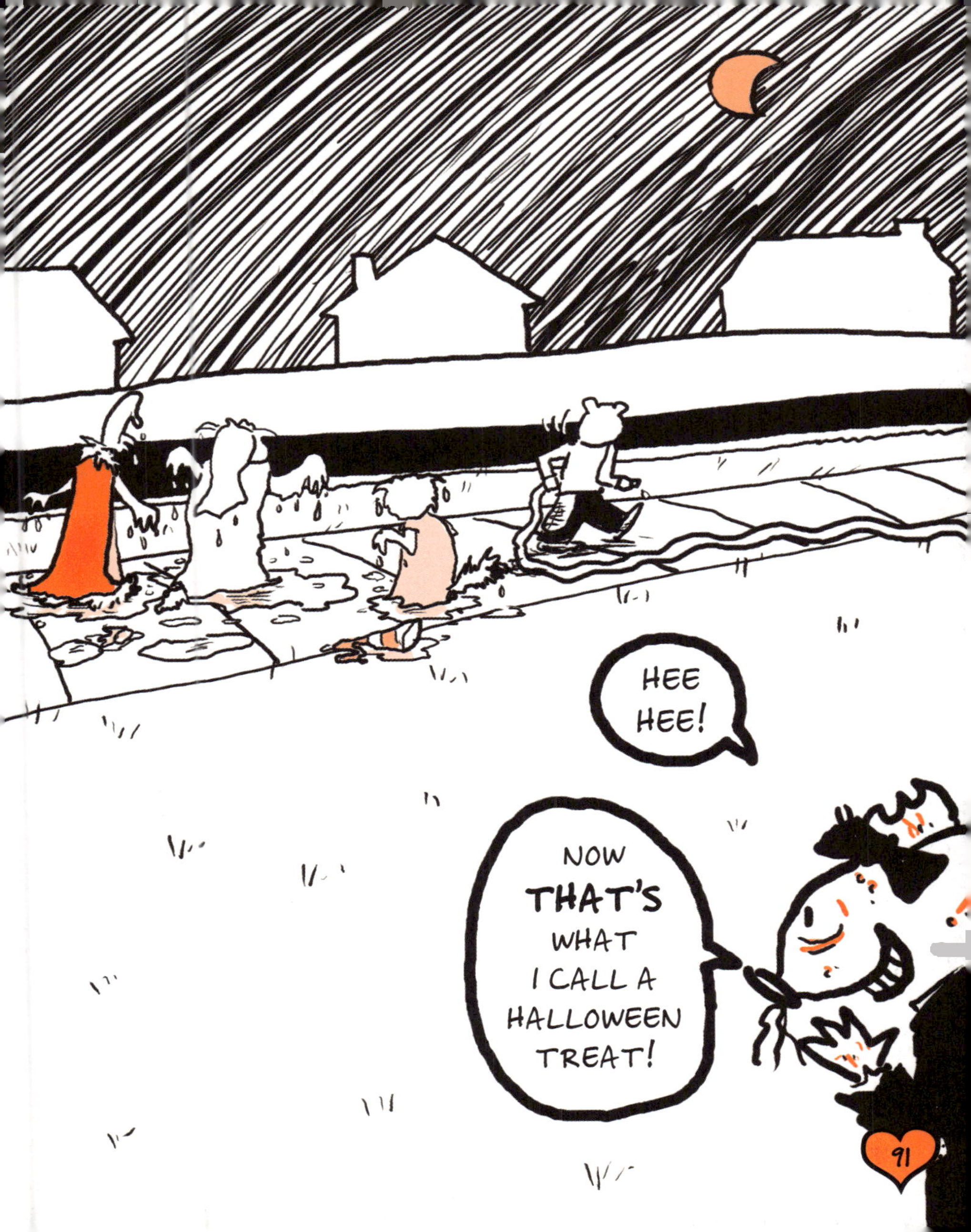
HEE HEE!
NOW THAT'S WHAT I CALL A HALLOWEEN TREAT!

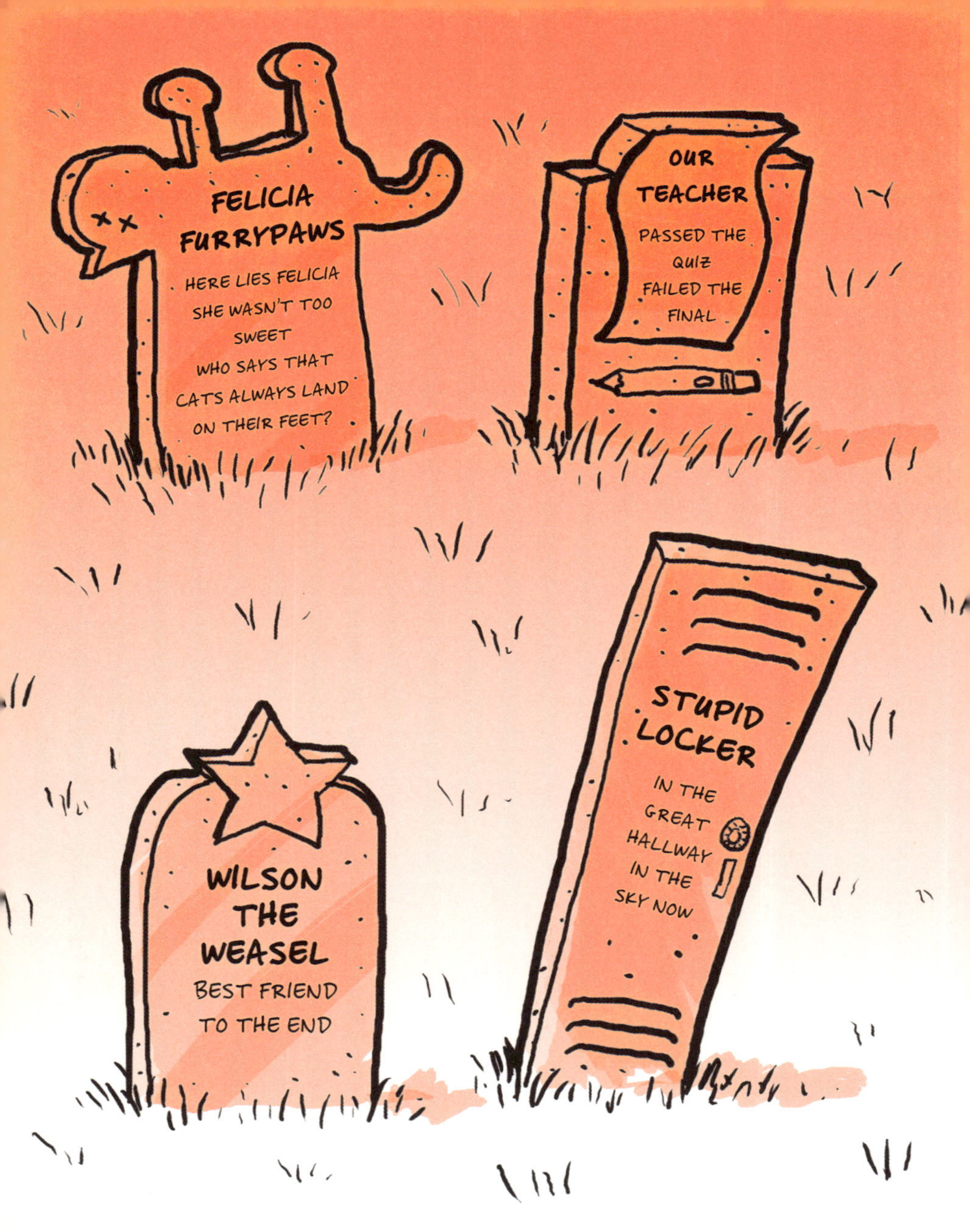
FELICIA FURRYPAWS
HERE LIES FELICIA SHE WASN'T TOO SWEET WHO SAYS THAT CATS ALWAYS LAND ON THEIR FEET?
OUR TEACHER
PASSED THE QUIZ FAILED THE FINAL
WILSON THE WEASEL
BEST FRIEND TO THE END
STUPID LOCKER
IN THE GREAT HALLWAY IN THE SKY NOW

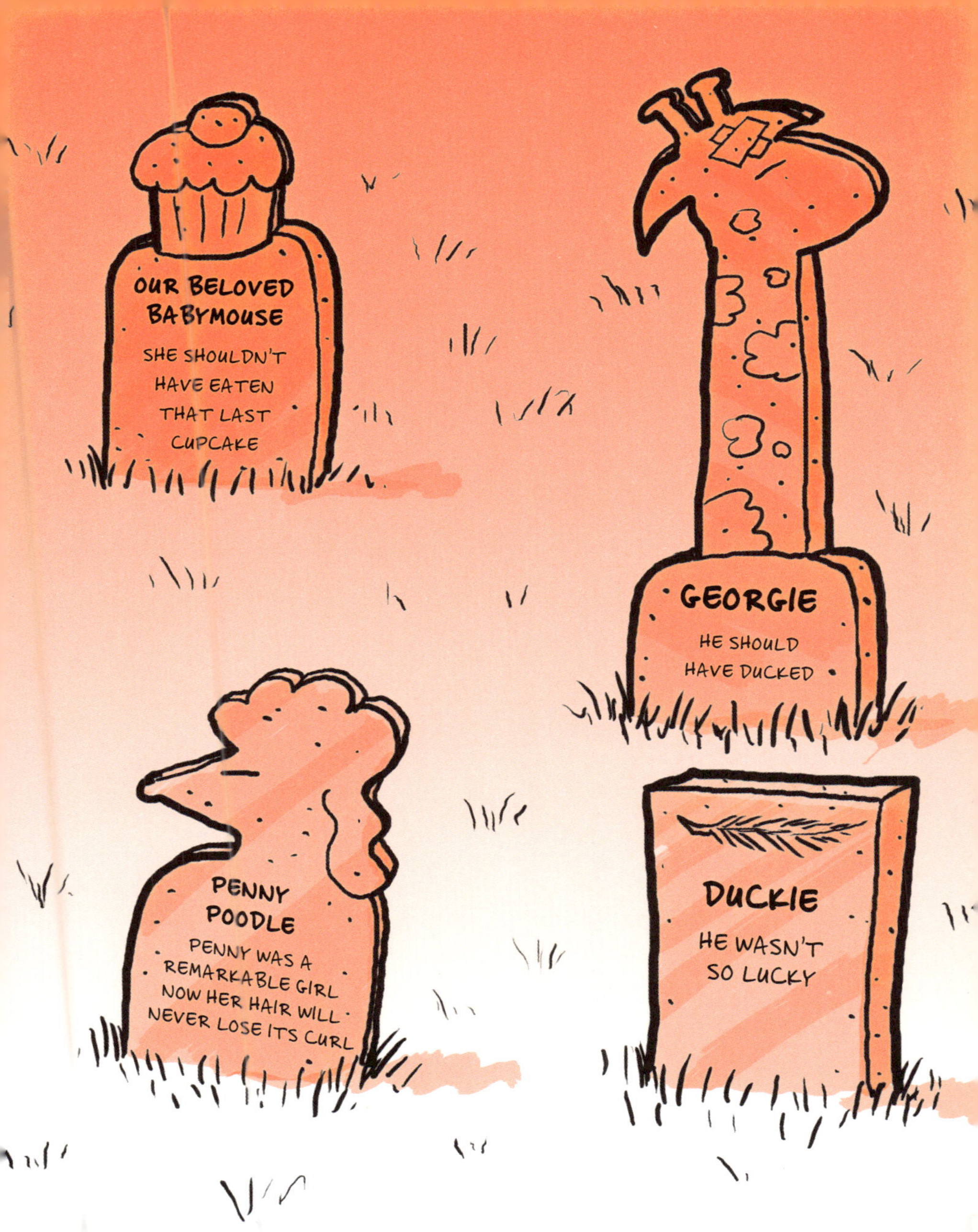

OUR BELOVED BABYMOUSE
SHE SHOULDN'T HAVE EATEN THAT LAST CUPCAKE
GEORGIE
HE SHOULD HAVE DUCKED
PENNY POODLE
PENNY WAS A REMARKABLE GIRL NOW HER HAIR WILL NEVER LOSE ITS CURL
DUCKIE
HE WASN'T SO LUCKY

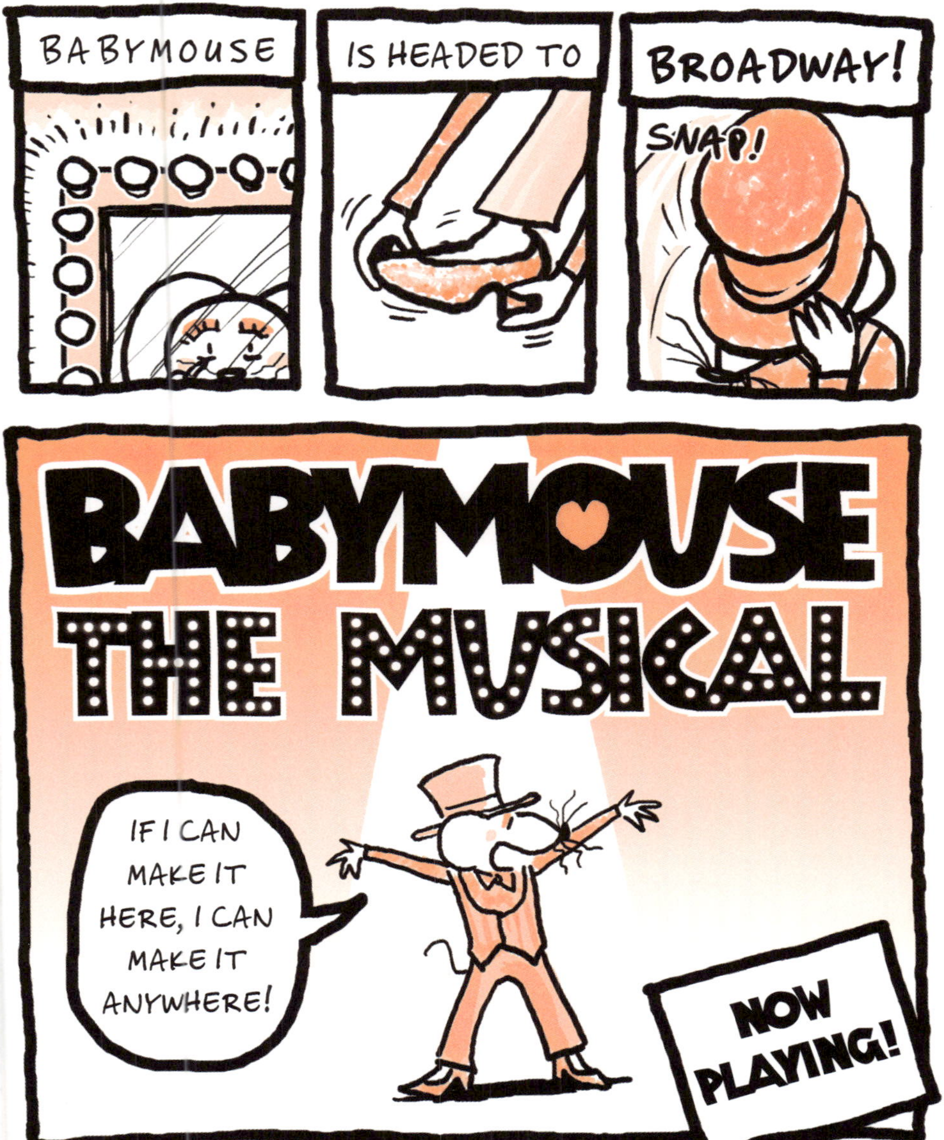
BABYMOUSE
IS HEADED TO
BROADWAY!
SNAP!
BABYMOUSE
THE MUSICAL
IF I CAN MAKE IT HERE, I CAN MAKE IT ANYWHERE!
NOW PLAYING!